COMMANDER

SIENNA SNOW

POLITICS OF LOVE

COMMANDER

THE POLITICS OF LOVE
BOOK 3

Sienna Snow

CHAPTER ONE

Fifteen years ago

"What do you mean it's over?" The devastation on Ashur Kumar's face ripped my heart to shreds.

He stood against the shadow of the setting sun in Houston's Memorial Park. The trees protected us from the sweltering August heat, but my body shook as if chilled to the bone.

Wrapping my arms around myself, I continued with the words that would damn me for the rest of my life. The words that would irrevocably break two hearts forever.

"Exactly what I said. You had to know this wouldn't last beyond the summer. I leave for Boston in a matter of days. You are going to take over your father's company. Long-distance relationships are destined to fail."

My throat burned as if were coated with acid.

If only I could tell him the truth. But if Ashur got one inkling that his father, Minesh Kumar, was forcing me to leave him, I wouldn't have a future. My family wouldn't have a future. And no matter how much I loved Ashur, I couldn't sacrifice my parents. They were good people who worked hard but hadn't been born with a silver spoon.

Men with money and power held all the cards, and those of us without means had no choice but to follow along or get demolished. It had no bearing that I had scholarships for academic success. A few choice words from a wealthy donor and all my future ambitions would disappear.

I wiped the tears streaming down my cheeks.

"So, in other words, you used me. Just like Papa said you'd use me."

What? That bastard had told Ashur this. I should have known something was up when I'd felt Ashur pulling away from me.

How could he believe I'd do that?

"No. It's nothing like what he said."

"Bullshit," he snapped. "Then why are you doing this?"

"Ashu, I wish it didn't have to be this way."

"Did you ever love me, or was everything you ever said a lie?"

"I never lied to you." I wrung my hands together.

"You found someone else. Admit it and make it easier on us."

How could he believe there was anyone else in my life? He was the one and only man I'd ever loved or would ever love.

I shook my head. "No, it has nothing to do with anyone, but..."

"Papa says he has proof. I refused to see it, but now I wonder."

Proof? What proof?

When I wasn't working as a clerk at a local pharmacy, I was taking core curriculum classes at the local university so I could save on tuition when I went to Harvard. When the hell would I have had time to cheat on Ashur?

God, I couldn't do this. I couldn't lie to him this way. I had to tell him the truth.

There had to be a way to figure out how to make it through the fallout.

Dad had told me he didn't care about the job, that he and Mom would survive without the high-salaried position. He'd said they'd move anywhere, as long as no one interfered with my dreams.

I'd been so scared about the future that I hadn't doubted that Minesh Kumar would do something to jeopardize my enrollment at Harvard.

You are such an idiot, Tara. You walked right into his web.

"Ashu, please listen to me."

"The person I should have listened to was Papa."

"No, that's not true. It's all a lie. I don't want to do this." I clenched my fists, not knowing how to fix this.

"Do what? Make me feel like I mattered? Make me believe it was about me and not my money? I'm done."

"Please," I begged. "Look past the facade he's created. He isn't the man you think he is. He told me if—"

"Go, Tara." Ashur cut me off. "I hope the new fish you've found makes you happy."

"Please let me explain." I grabbed his arm, but he shook me off.

"I don't want to hear another word," he bit out. "I would have given you the world. You were my everything. Damn you. I'll never forgive you for this."

He turned, leaving me at the edge of the park.

I closed my eyes and slid to the ground, trying to hold in pain like I'd never felt before.

***

Present Day

"You have your instructions. After this last mission, I am no longer in charge of Solon-North

America," I said to the men and women around the conference table.

I'd led this group of agents for the past five years, and to them my word was law. Soon, they'd take directions from someone else, a person just as capable, if not more. But for me, it meant my life was forever changed.

No going back now, Tara. You knew what you were getting into. Now you have to live with it.

"Will you be returning to your role or is this a permanent leave?"

I expected this question, and I wasn't sure how to answer it. Should I give the politically correct response a woman in my situation would relay by saying I was permanently retired, or give them the one that they expected, knowing the type of person I was?

"My future role is one that will have many restrictions, limiting my usefulness in any capacity for the time being."

I knew my response wasn't satisfying to anyone, but it was the only one I could give. I couldn't predict what the future held for me or what I would be able to do once I left Washington. But for the next I-didn't-know-how-many years, 1600 Pennsylvania Ave. was my home, and my life would be in the public eye. As if it wasn't already. But if it meant I could save countless lives, so be it.

A beep from my smartwatch sounded, telling me my security detail would be arriving any moment and to wrap up the meeting.

"Thank you, everyone. It has been a pleasure working with all of you."

With those last words, the room emptied with the exception of one person, Tyler Camden. He was the current Secretary of State and the new director of Solon, a secret organization focused on stopping human trafficking throughout the world.

He leaned against a wall while watching me.

Ignoring him, I walked over to the third-story windows of my building and stared out at the unobstructed view of the White House.

The countdown to the moment that would seal the course of the rest of my life was now in its final stage, and I had less than seventy-two hours of freedom left. After which, my existence would become even more confined than it had been for the last year and a half.

"Commander Zain. Are you sure you want to do this? It isn't too late to back out of the wedding."

I turned from the view and glared at Tyler.

"What? Did I say something wrong, Commander?"

Tyler and I had developed a friendship as young college graduates recruited into Solon while going through our initial training in the organization. Later we'd worked as partners in various assignments before parting ways and pursuing vastly different public careers. He'd gone the way of politics as any conservative third-generation Louisiana politician would go, and I'd gone the route of human rights attorney, taking on every controversial case that brought light to the plague of so many people in the world.

His blondish brown hair was a bit messy, and the sleeves of his button-down shirt were rolled up to the elbow. He looked like an ad for some expensive menswear catalog. Tyler was one of the most handsome men I had ever met, second only to the one I'd wed in a matter of days. Aside from his looks, Tyler possessed an uncanny intellect that allowed him to move between the worlds of the polite elite and underground societies.

"That isn't funny, Mr. Secretary," I responded. "I thought you'd leave with the team."

Tyler smirked as he came around the table to stand next to me. He enjoyed reminding me daily that I could change my mind about stepping down. As far as he knew, I had never been the marrying type, and whatever my fiancé was offering me to marry him wasn't worth it. Tyler wanted me to marry for love.

What Tyler couldn't understand was that I'd loved once before and I'd never risk my heart again. And the best way to prevent another heartbreak was to marry the very man who'd shattered my belief in fairy tales and happily ever after.

"But Commander, the troops will never be the same without you."

"Stop saying that or I'll punch you," I growled. "You know how much I hate that title?"

I was never going to live down the name a combatant had given me during a contentious negotiation. The man had tried his hardest to intimidate me, thinking that pointing a gun in my face would scare me into complying with his demands.

Well, it had scared me, but I'd trained myself not to react. After all, I had a habit of walking into situations that had a potential to cause an international incident.

When I'd calmly informed the man that his compound was surrounded by my army of hired guns who wouldn't hesitate to protect me, he laughed and said I was a worthy opponent even if I was a woman.

"What title?"

"Tyler," I warned. "Can it with the Commander shit. I have enough on my mind as it is. Let me have these last moments in my office without thinking about the circus that has become my life."

I turned my gaze to the flawless diamond surrounded by sapphires adorning the ring finger of my left hand and shuddered.

Could I do this? Could I be with Ashur Minesh Kumar, the most powerful man in the nation? Could I become first lady without fucking it up? Could I sleep with a man who made me remember the past but didn't love me? Could never love me?

My gaze moved to the cover of a news magazine. A polished couple stared out from the pages. The man with rich chocolate eyes, breathtaking good looks, and impeccably groomed style stood with a petite woman who barely came up to his shoulder. There was a headline that read, "First comes an election, then comes marriage, will babies be next?"

A prickle of goosebumps broke out over my skin.

"If you agree to marry me and start a new political dynasty, I will happily sign over half my fortune."

"What do you mean, start a political dynasty?"

"Exactly what I said. I want children. Help me win the election, give me two children, and you can save the world with your endeavors without ever worrying about funding again."

"So, you want me to give you petri dish children? That doesn't sound too bad."

"No, Tara. I want them the old-fashioned way."

Tyler set a hand on my shoulder, pulling me from my thoughts. "Commander is who you are, Tara. The agent who will take down an assailant before they knew what hit them. The negotiator who will face off against the scum of the earth to save one life. The woman who is willing to move heaven and earth to help a friend. Just in case you've forgotten, with all the chaos of the election and now the wedding, I thought I'd remind you of who you are."

If Tyler only knew that my marriage would allow me to continue my public human rights work until the day I died. Then again, he couldn't know. That clause was part of the deal—no one outside of my fiancé and his best friend, Veer George, the current vice president, would ever have any inkling of the details of my relationship.

Eighteen months ago, when we'd agreed to the bargain, love was the last thing on our minds.

Ashur needed a wife, one who would balance his very conservative-leaning tendencies and make him appeal to the voters the then-sitting ultra-conservative president, Henry Edgar, had alienated.

According to Ashur, I was the perfect candidate as an uber-left-wing save-the-world liberal. Especially since I'd navigated a situation where I'd gone toe to toe with Edgar and come out the hero and more internationally renowned than ever. Then there was the fact that we had been childhood sweethearts. This part of our history would give the storybook second-chance romantic solidification to our relationship.

Ashur had offered me fifty percent of his net worth in exchange for marrying him. What he hadn't known was that I was fully funded by Solon and could do my various humanitarian projects without a second thought.

I'd agreed to his proposal because I needed power. Especially the power that came with a high net worth and allowed me into circles only the elite could ever hope of being included. Among this group of people hid the financiers of the operations that I'd made my life goal to stop.

"You're one to talk, Mr. Secretary of State. Last I checked, your position as my eyes and ears on the ground disappeared the day you accepted your new job."

"What was I supposed to say? Ashur is the first president in history to truly fill all high-level positions with people from all political associations and not just his. I'm more useful now than I ever was before."

"So am I." I lifted my chin in challenge but knew the lie for what it was. I'd become the pretty face behind the man. A role I'd never ever thought I'd fill.

"That is the furthest thing from the truth, and you know it." He dropped his arm and turned his gaze to the ominous building down the street from us. "No one will question why I'm meeting with leaders of international organizations or heads of state. It will be a requirement of my job. You, on the other hand, live under a microscope. You are the American version of rags-to-riches to first lady. Everything and anything you do will forever be scrutinized."

"I know." I sighed. "The days of making midnight runs for pizza and ice cream are things of the past."

"I'm sure you could still do those things. Albeit with an audience."

"The last thing I'll want to do is to put on a full face of makeup and look pristine to go get some comfort food. I'd need a ringmaster to control the chaos."

"You do realize, your marriage would have been less of

a media circus if you'd decided to tie the knot before he took office?" He rubbed a thumb under my eye. "You look exhausted."

"If I'd done that then this last assignment wouldn't be feasible. With the American people focused on me and the 'American wedding of the century'—" I air quoted, "—the team can implement our plan."

A slight tremor ran up my spine as I peeked toward the Secret Service agents discreetly positioned outside my door. My privacy had become all but nonexistent the second the election results had come in last fall.

At least the head of my security was an agent in Solon and understood my need for discretion. Whenever I "worked," he'd make sure I was given enough space so I wouldn't break attorney-client privilege. Well, that was the excuse given to the rest of my protection detail.

"It's dangerous and could place all of us in the middle of a scandal bigger than anything we've ever faced. Are you sure it's worth it? There are other ways."

"There are no other ways," I countered. "Ameera Kamini sacrificed her safety countless times to help us. The least we can do is help her escape the web she was caught in because of us."

Three months ago, my best friend and fellow Solon agent had been kidnapped by a terrorist organization known for human trafficking. They'd assumed she was an American spy and decided to auction her for the information she knew. I'd entered the auction as a potential bidder under an assumed name I'd used during various operations. The only stipulation I had to meet was to show a net worth of over one hundred million. With the money I'd get from Ashur I qualified. Now we were in a wait-and-see mode. The date was set for two weeks from now, but the place and exact time of the bidding was still unknown.

"It has the potential to cause an international incident if we don't time this right."

"Not if you do your part and I do mine. Once she is on US soil again, I can relax."

It killed me that Ameera wouldn't be part of the wedding. Even worse was not knowing where she was. We'd followed countless leads, but by the time my agents reached her, Ameera's captors had moved to a new location.

"No, that's when the trouble's going to start. The story of her being on assignment is only going to work for a few more weeks. We're lucky no one has grown suspicious since she has a history of living out of the country for long periods of time."

"We've had the decoy checking in. As far as anyone knows she's on assignment in South Africa. We'll make sure to debrief her on her reports before she goes back in."

"Tara, we don't know what condition she'll be in when we find her. She may never go back."

"She's strong. No matter what happens, she won't break."

I had to believe this—the alternative was unthinkable.

"We have another problem to navigate. Actually, two problems."

"What?" I asked.

"Her father has entered the auction."

I clenched my teeth. "How do you know? And how the fuck did he find out she was missing?"

Ameera was the daughter of Hamir Ustaf, the self-proclaimed king of Janestan, a small country near India and Pakistan. Nearly thirty years ago, while attending Princeton, he'd had a one-night stand with Ameera's mother, Nicola Kamini, a fashion model. Ameera had never met Hamir and wanted nothing to do with him.

As far as the world was concerned, Nicola's husband, Travis Angelo, was her biological father.

It wasn't until she was twenty-five and working at the UN as a foreign relations specialist that she'd met Hamir. He'd expected her to accept him with open arms but was shocked when she'd informed him that any contact with her could result in arrest for his crimes against humanity.

What Hamir hadn't known was she worked for Solon and was aware of everything he'd done from the time he'd left the university until he'd become the dictator. He was the poster boy for the type of people Solon fought against.

Needless to say, Hamir hadn't taken the slight well and

had vowed to make her see the correct way to treat her father.

Tyler looked out the window and ran a hand through his hair. "The same way we found out they're auctioning Ameera."

The dark web. This hidden portion of the web was scoured by Solon agents continuously and was how we conducted most of our operations.

"Ustaf has created a counter auction to find his daughter and bring her to him."

"So, he's going to buy her, just to sell her in marriage to the most useful bidder?"

Tyler clenched his jaw, and his normally happy blue eyes grew hard. "I'll get her out."

The determination in his voice told me I wasn't the only one who cared for Ameera. Solon agents were a family, a makeshift family of mercenaries, but a family nonetheless. However, Tyler and Ameera had a history, one that went into the realm beyond lovers but not quite a couple.

"What's the second problem?"

"There's an unknown third buyer. We've scoured the net but can't find any information on them."

"Keep looking. We can't risk anyone but us getting to Ameera."

Between this wedding and Ameera, I was at my limit of stress.

"So, are you ever going to tell your fiancé what you truly do for a living?"

Not if I could help it. How does one tell the President of the United States that his wife is part of a secret organization with no loyalty to any country, that aims to stop human trafficking across the world and will use any means—some that aren't always legal—to get it done?

I folded my arms across my body. "Are you going to tell your family that you aren't only the strictly by-the-books and too-pretty-for-his-own-good Southern politician?"

"Not the same, Tara, and you know it."

"How is it not the same?" I asked defensively.

"I'm not the one marrying the President of the United States. Hell, I may never get married if you don't stop sending me on do-or-die assignments."

"You would have gotten bored without me. How else would you get to live out your fantasy of being a secret agent?"

Tyler grunted as he rubbed his shoulder on the spot scarred by a gunshot wound. "It isn't a fantasy if I'm living it."

"You won't have to worry about that anymore after we get Ameera back. Then, I'll no longer be the head honcho. You will." I smiled.

"A job I got because you decided to get hitched. Some friend you are," he joked, then all of a sudden his tone changed. "Seriously, Tara. Ashur can help you. He'll want to help you if you tell him. He is former military and owns a technology company that could help us. You can trust him. He'll stand by you. Plus, Ameera technically works for him, and he could head off any fallout from getting her back in the US."

Trust. That was a loaded word. Trust meant I had faith Ashur would stand by me no matter what happened. Trust meant he would fight for me even when the lie was more believable than the truth. I trusted very few people to have my back, and Ashur wasn't one of them.

He'd professed he loved me but hadn't fought for me. He'd walked away, never questioning anything that was going on around him or why someone behaved the way they had.

"It's better he doesn't know. Plausible deniability and all that."

"Yeah, right. You still haven't gotten over what happened when the both of you were kids."

"I was over that shit years ago," I lied and then added, "An eighteen- and twenty-three-year-old aren't kids."

"I do believe you protest too much. Tara, you can trust him."

"I wouldn't marry a man I didn't trust with my future. You should know this."

"But what about your heart and your secrets? He needs someone to lean on as much as you do."

"Whatever," I mumbled, pushing down the need to

deny the truth of Tyler's words and deciding to change the subject. "My leave is only temporary, despite what I said to the group."

I shifted, jostling the side table next to me and knocking a vase over.

I snatched it before it hit the floor and set it back on the table, which resulted in a lifted brow from Tyler.

"Okay, that wasn't a subtle change of subject at all." Tyler snorted. "There is no way possible for you to come back to the same role. You can't go risking your life the way you've done in the past. Your marriage with Ashur will no doubt include children and happy little Secret Service agents following you around everywhere you go for the rest of your life. Better get those reflexes under control too. Most people aren't trained the way we are."

"You're such an ass."

"Tell me I'm wrong, and I'll tell you that you're delusional."

I was saved from responding as a knock came from the door. Both Tyler and I looked toward my security lead, Casey Adler.

"Ms. Zain. Your vehicle is ready to take you for your final fitting."

"And the circus recommences," Tyler said and offered me his arm as I exited my DC law office for the last time.

CHAPTER TWO

An hour after leaving my office, I stepped out of my limo into a swarm of paparazzi lining the street outside of my designer friend Shawna Martinez's DC showroom. My security team surrounded me, keeping the media a safe distance away. The normally twenty-minute drive was hindered by crowds at every turn. Someone from either the White House or Shawna's staff had tipped off the news outlets that I'd be at the shop, and everyone wanted that last-minute picture of the bride-to-be and a possible peek at the wedding outfit.

No one knew that Shawna wasn't the one designing my dress. In fact, I wasn't wearing a dress at all. I planned to wear a traditional Indian wedding *lengha*. A three-piece ivory silk outfit embroidered with heavy silver beading as well as gold and intricate red stitching. I loved my heritage and wanted to add a piece of it to the very American-style wedding Ashur and I would have in less than three days' time. I'd had a total of four outfits custom made for my short frame. Each ensemble made me feel gorgeous, a requirement for any woman about to walk down the aisle.

A small part of me was sad that I wouldn't get the traditional Indian wedding I'd dreamed of since I was a kid with all the festivities and family and chaos. However, another part of me was glad—a modern wedding that was the polar opposite of what I wanted would keep me focused on the fact my marriage wasn't anything more than a business agreement. I couldn't afford to think otherwise, or I'd get tangled up in the emotions I'd locked away that long-ago summer.

A flash of camera lights snapped me out of my thoughts and made me growl inside.

"Ms. Zain, this way," Casey said as we made our way into the building.

The second the doors closed, he gestured to the other agents to close the window shades of the shop.

A loud groan echoed through the glass.

Oh, the poor nosy papz would have to wait to get any more pictures. Maybe I should throw them a bone.

Not!

Tyler was right—gone were the days of midnight food runs or outings to dance clubs to meet up with friends on my days off from assignments. Now my life would be filled with meetings, charities, and galas.

I swallowed. Jesus. I wasn't refined enough for this life. I was too opinionated, too bossy, and too liberal.

Why the fuck Ashur thought I'd make a great first lady was beyond me.

No matter what he'd pitched I knew better than to believe that without me he'd never win the election. I was probably more a liability than an asset.

My incident with the former president hadn't been my first headline-making scandal. But it had been the most taxing. And the one that could have landed me in jail.

Ashur wanted something from me outside of sex that I hadn't figured out yet, and I was the dumbass who'd agreed to marry him without all the facts. Whatever it was, it was too late to change my mind. Ashur and I were bound together for the rest of our lives.

And don't forget, you need Ashur's money to free Ameera.

At that moment, my phone rang. I paused in a hallway and reached into my purse. Taking a peek at the caller ID, I sighed. Of course, he'd call when I was thinking of him.

"Hello, Mr. President."

"Hello, First Lady." Ashur's deep, raspy voice washed over me. "How is the fitting going?"

"It hasn't started, and for the record, I'm not first lady yet," I said a little too breathlessly.

What the fuck, Tara? How was I going to keep it

businesslike when the sound of his voice made me think about things I should keep locked away?

"The ceremony is only a technicality. We've been legally wed for nearly two years now."

"Most of the world doesn't know this, including our families." I tucked a stray hair behind my ear.

As part of our agreement, we'd legally wed a week after I'd agreed to marry Ashur. Marrying him meant there was no backing out, for him or me.

"I know and you know." There was a tinge of possessiveness in his tone that made my heart beat a little faster.

"Ashur."

"Ashu," he countered.

I bit my lip and then responded. "You told me never to call you that, remember?"

He'd said those words out of hurt and anger, but the pain still lingered. It had been my pet name for him when we were young and stupid. Before the family interferences and the betrayals and the loss of my innocence and the view that the world wouldn't let the bad guys win.

"I said only my lover could say that name. You are my lover, Tara."

His words sent a shiver down my spine.

"Not yet."

"Soon. I've kept to our bargain but know this: once

we're together, you'll crave me as much as I crave you. Sex was the only thing we got right."

The desire lacing his words made my skin tingle and a pulse of need flare to life.

"Don't you have a country to run? Stop thinking about sex and get back to work."

"I'm good at multitasking." He chuckled, bringing a smile to my lips. He rarely, if ever, laughed.

After we'd broken up, Ashur had turned down his position in Kumar Technologies, the billion-dollar software firm his father owned, and joined the Air Force and then deployed to Afghanistan. By the time he returned from his second tour, he was a changed man. The easy-to-smile boy had disappeared, replaced by a too-focused man who only saw things in black and white, right and wrong.

"Was there a reason you called, Mr. President? I'm positive clothing details are the last things you're concerned with."

"Did I tell you that I enjoyed our discussion the other day?"

"You mean the one where you said I was too much of a bleeding-heart liberal to understand the nuances of the costs associated with implementing the immigration bill with the provisions the Democrats wanted?"

Another laugh sounded over the line. "Yes, that one. I wanted to say thank you."

I shifted the phone to my other ear. "For what?"

The last thing I'd expect was a thank-you for a discussion that had turned so heated I'd walked out.

"For giving me a sounding board and a perspective that was different from mine."

"Oh."

"It helped me compromise today, and instead of an eight-hour meeting as scheduled, it was only three."

"Well, I'm glad I could help."

"Maybe one day I can return the favor."

Before I could respond, a voice called out to Ashur, and he sighed.

"I have to go. See you tonight for the parental gathering."

"I'm going to have a cocktail or two before I get there."

"So will I. So will I."

"Goodbye, Ashur."

"Goodbye, First Lady." He hung up.

I shook my head. That man could be cold and emotionless one minute and then flirty and sweet the next.

We'd been polar opposites from the beginning. Although we had one particular thing in common—our mutual dread of being in the same room with Ashur's father. Minesh Kumar was unpleasant on a good day. When he was in a piss-poor mood, people considered jumping from a window to escape the drama.

I stuffed my phone back in my bag and turned the

corner to the private dressing area in Shawna's store that was reserved for all her VIP clients.

"Hey there." Samina Kumar-Camden greeted me and then handed me a glass of champagne. Sam, as we liked to call her, was my law partner in our Seattle firm, the junior senator from Washington state, and my sister-in-law.

"I so needed this. Where is everyone?"

"Jacinta is running late from a finance committee meeting, and Shawna is on her way with Neya and our outfits."

"Good. I need a few moments without thinking about this wedding." *Or sex with your brother*, I wanted to add but decided to keep that bit to myself.

"Did something happen?"

I drank down the whole glass and then answered, "This media attention is a bit overwhelming. I can't burp without someone picking it up on a high-definition microphone."

Sam snorted and then laughed. "Can you imagine how many times they'd replay the sound bite? I suggest you keep those type of bodily functions under wraps. Wait until they follow you into the bathroom."

I glared at her but smirked, holding my glass up for a refill. "You are so not funny. At least people would think I'm human and not the robot some of the news agencies have dubbed me."

"They stopped saying that after they got those pictures

of you looking at Ash during the inaugural ball. They do call him your Achilles' heel."

"Whatever," I grumbled.

Sam filled my flute to the top and returned the bottle to the chilling bucket. "Besides, those are tabloids. Who cares?"

"I do. You, Miss Celebrity Attorney with all of Hollywood begging to be your client, know how to use the spotlight to your advantage. I, on the other hand, come out looking like a frosty bitch because I refuse to throw them a bone."

"Former celebrity attorney. I'm a respectable United States senator now." Sam took a sip of her drink.

"Does Devin know this? If I recall, I'm the one who caught you two fucking on the couch of my newly renovated office. I think you scarred me for life. You're lucky it was only me and not Ashur who walked in on you."

Sam waved her hand as if it wasn't a big deal and sat down on a burgundy-fabric-covered armchair. "It's not like it would be the first time this happened to Ash. Besides. I hadn't seen my hubby in weeks with both our crazy travel schedules. I am the mother of two toddlers that suck every ounce of energy out of me the moment I step foot into our house, so we have to get it when we can."

"See this face." I pointed to mine. "No sympathy

whatsoever. I feel like my brain needs to be bleached of the memory."

"Just you wait. One day you and Ashur will want a quickie between meetings and running the country, and you'll willingly risk someone catching you for a round of hot sex."

I collapsed on a white couch across from Samina and set my feet on the mirrored coffee table.

The idea of sex with Ashur brought heat to my core. I knew from past experience, he was an incredible lover. I'd given him my virginity as a barely grown girl with stars in my eyes. Even then, there was always a way about his presence that made my body burn with a need to be touched. Now it was even more intense than before. The barest sound of his voice and my cleft flooded with desire.

Maybe I should have jumped him. Then I wouldn't feel this pull for him every time I was near him.

I snorted inside. Who was I kidding?

Once Ashur and I started the sexual aspect of our relationship again, there was no doubt we'd fuck every chance we got. We'd probably give Samina and Devin a run for their money.

The last year and a half had built on a sexual undercurrent that had always existed between Ashur and me. I'd pretend to feel nothing and keep a "too cool for school" attitude. But everyone around us could feel the tension, especially Ashur. There was always a slight tug at his lips that would tell me he noticed my reaction to him. Something that made me want to punch him and kiss him.

God, I hadn't kissed him in forever. Yes, I'd pecked him for a brief moment in front of the media but nothing intimate. Not even during our quiet civil ceremony in his office. The sad part was that even the barest graze of his lips caused me to want to throw caution to the wind and seal the deal.

Thankfully, Ashur had kept to his word about keeping our relationship platonic until we "officially" married.

Sex would complicate things in a way that I worried I wouldn't be able to keep things unemotional. Physical intimacy was something I shared with a person I loved, and I could never mistake what would happen with Ashur as anything other than quenching sexual need.

Ashur had made it clear love was something he'd never feel for me again. I'd ripped his heart in two, and he'd never gotten over it.

Shit. Why am I wallowing in this? I know what I've agreed to. Hell, I was the one who drew up the contract.

"Ahh, I got you thinking. Please do me a favor. Lock the door whenever I'm around. No matter what I say. I don't want to see my brother boning one of my best friends."

Thank God for Sam. She had a way with words that kept me from thinking too much.

"Don't worry. The Secret Service would stop you

before you encountered a surprise." I glanced at Casey, who was pretending he hadn't heard anything we'd talked about.

"I'm sure they have plenty of stories to tell but are sworn to secrecy." Samina studied me as she made her comment. "Tara, I have a question for you."

"Shoot," I said, lifting my glass to my lips and then taking another deep gulp.

"Why aren't you fucking my brother? A person has to be dead not to see the chemistry between you two. Is 'no sex' part of the bargain Ashur made with you?"

I coughed, nearly choking on my champagne. How the fuck would she know about my deal with Ashur? He'd stipulated that no one was to know anything other than that we fell back in love.

"What makes y—?"

"Don't even try that deflection shit. I am a master at that game."

I sighed, set my glass on the table, and leaned back on the couch, pinching the bridge of my nose. "It's complicated."

"Every couple has issues. Hey, look at Dev and me. We worked through our problems and are happier than we've ever been."

She had a point. For years, Samina and Devin's relationship was a secret. Sam being a celebrity attorney and a celebrity in her own right would have been detrimental to Devin's and his father's careers. So, for over a decade, they kept quiet about who they were to each other, even going as far as dating other people.

It took Samina filing for divorce for Devin to get his act in gear and work his best to win her back. After a lot of work, the two of them were one of the most solid couples I knew and the proud parents of two beautiful children.

"It's different on a whole new level. You and Dev never stopped loving each other."

"Neither have the two of you."

I opened my eyes and gaped at her. "Sorry, but you are way off base. I loved Ashur for a long time after we broke up. It wasn't until three years later when I started dating Xander that I got over him."

Xander Alexi was a man who'd given me what I'd needed to get over Ashur. He was a friend, a confidant, a study partner, and for a brief time, a lover. We'd known what we had wouldn't last longer than our years at Harvard, Xander having to return to Greece to take over his family's business and me moving to California to attend law school at Stanford. To this day we remained friends with me serving as groom's lady at his wedding.

"I'm sure dating an international supermodel and shipping heir can do that to a girl."

"Whatever, I had no idea of his net worth until we were dating for a few months, and besides, you're the one who introduced us. Our dates were never fancy. We were broke college kids who loved to hang out, study, and eat pizza."

"Are y'all really talking about ex-boyfriends when there is a wedding in less than three days?" Jacinta Camden-George, the junior senator from Texas and wife of the vice president, asked as she walked in from a back room with Shawna and Neya Sunkureddi. They all carried boxes, which I could assume contained my many outfits and accessories.

Neya was a former partner turned friend, who happened to be a well-known fashion designer in India. When she'd offered to design my wedding outfits, I'd jumped at the chance. Outside of her work for international affairs, she was one of the most sought-after fashion designers in Indian haute couture.

I smiled at everyone and then pointed to Sam. "She brought it up. I was merely an innocent bystander."

Jacinta glared at Samina. "She's about to marry your brother, the president, and there are like a million reporters out front. The last thing the two of you need to do is talk about hot exes with unending bank accounts when someone could be hiding to record any conversations."

Sam winced—no one wanted to get on Jacinta's bad side, especially after a four-hour Senate Finance Committee meeting. And the fact Jacinta was six months pregnant only added to the grumpiness.

"Sorry. I promise never to bring up Tara's hot-as-fuck ex again."

Shaking my head, I said, "Sam, you know I love you, but you are a complete pain in the ass."

"Torturing my *Bhabhi* is a privilege I plan to use to the fullest. You've always been my sister, but now it will be official."

My heart contracted to hear her refer to me with the traditional Gujarati word for a sister-in-law. Sam and I had had a bond since we were young. She was the prodigy daughter of a billionaire, and I was the awkward tween daughter of a worker in her father's company. We ran in different circles—Sam in the world of privilege and social standing and me in the life of limited income and saving pennies. But somehow, we'd always found each other. Especially during social events, where we never fit in and wanted to escape the pretense. We'd end up sitting in some hallway, chatting about nonsensical stuff and laughing our heads off.

When the drama between Ashur and me happened, she was dealing with her own issues with her father and her relationship with Devin and the last thing I wanted to do was burden her with my troubles. We'd stayed in touch over the years, but it wasn't until I entered law school and Samina was finishing up her last year that our bond had grown. Even though we were only a few months apart in age, she'd became my mentor and even helped me get my first job after Stanford.

Then about seven years ago, we'd joined forces to start our own law firm. Sometimes, I still couldn't believe the success we'd achieved in such a short time. I knew some of it was due to the clients Solon had referred to the firm, but no one, including Samina, knew that tidbit of information.

"I guess that means I can boss you around like the older brother's wife does in Bollywood movies," I said to Sam.

"And how would this be any different than normal?" Sam muttered, making Jacinta, Shawna, and Neya laugh. "You'd give Attila the Hun a run for his money."

"Bite me." I picked up my glass again and took another deep sip. "I just like to make sure all I's are dotted and T's crossed."

"She's got you there." Neya set a box in front of me. "You've been a bossy boot since the moment I met you ten years ago. And with this wedding—you're lucky I love you. Otherwise I would have designed the ugliest lengha possible for being such a micromanager."

"You're one to talk, miss. I will cut you if anyone touches my designs." I sat up and began to open the box Neya brought me. "Let's get this fitting underway. I'm due for a family dinner with the in-laws."

Sam groaned. "Don't remind me. I'm not sure I won't

stab the tech man. I'm going to drink at least three more glasses to increase my tolerance for his antics."

"He's your father."

"Thanks for the reminder."

I grinned at her and then poured us both another glass of champagne.

CHAPTER THREE

A little before seven in the evening, I cleared security, and my car pulled up the private driveway leading to the entrance of the residence.

The fitting had turned into a lot more fun than I'd expected and included three more bottles of champagne. I was a little tipsy, with my senses dulled enough to handle the parental encounter awaiting me inside.

As an only child, I'd always wanted siblings, and my friends had turned into the family I dreamed of having. Those ladies would cut a bitch if anyone fucked with me.

I sighed.

If only Ameera was there, she'd have made it the ideal fitting. I missed her so much and couldn't stop the worry that constantly plagued me whenever I thought about her, which was often. When the girls had asked about her, I'd made up some excuse, saying she had to finish up a project in South Africa and couldn't get out of the assignment in time for the wedding. The girls were used to Ameera's international assignments that kept her out of the country for months at a times, so my excuse was believable. I hated lying, but what else was I supposed to do?

I was at the mercy of her captors, but if given the opportunity, I'd skip my wedding to get her back.

What sucked was that Ameera had only been in Geneva to resign from Solon. I was her North American director but we all reported to the international directing board who were in Geneva, and they required an in-person debriefing when tendering a resignation.

Years of working two time-consuming jobs had taken their toll on her, and she needed a change. One that wouldn't require espionage and always looking over her shoulder. Her goal was to take over her mother's fashion house and deal with the temperamental models instead of terrorists.

She'd never made it to her meeting. Instead, five minutes after she'd left her hotel, she was taken by the remaining members of a sleeper group Solon had brought down.

Now it was over three months later, and we still hadn't gotten her back. I could only hope and pray she was okay.

The car passed over a speed bump, jostling me out of my brooding.

I released a deep breath and pulled out my compact.

Time to get my game face on and ready myself to survive the night.

I could do it. Many people had in-law issues. I could deal with my father-in-law.

The door opened, and I scooted over. Casey offered me his hand as I stepped out.

"Is everyone here?" I asked Casey.

"I received word both families are waiting for you and Mr. Kumar in the Yellow Oval Room."

Straightening the pleats on my floor-length dress, I glanced toward the gardens. From my angle, I could see the windows of the Oval Office. Ashur would be in his meeting with the House Republicans.

Hopefully, the discussion would go smoothly, and they wouldn't run over. The last thing I wanted to do was be in a room with Minesh Kumar without Ashur. Minesh had turned my life upside down and ruined any chance of marrying for love.

I should have gotten over the past by now, but it was hard to do when the man took every opportunity to insult me and turn his nose up whenever I was in his vicinity.

I'd held my tongue for the last two years, wanting to keep the peace for Ashur's and Samina's sakes. They both had political careers where reporters and potential challengers were looking to find any dirt on their personal lives. Any whiff of my discourse with my father-in-law could lead to people snooping into my background more than they already had, and I had enough on my plate as it was.

"This way, Ms. Zain."

I studied Casey as I followed him through the entryway of the residence. He wasn't the only Solon agent I'd seen working in the White House since Ashur took office. Solon had men and women stationed in every government across the globe.

Yes, the organization's goal sounded idealistic, and maybe it was, but when any government had any say in an organization, there was always bureaucracy to slow things down. And what we did was time sensitive and could mean the difference between life and death. And then there was the fact that we toed the line of legal and illegal means of accomplishing our objectives.

Shit, I had to stop thinking I was still part of Solon. I couldn't afford the ramifications of anyone finding out what I'd spent my time doing for the last ten years.

A tall, middle-aged, balding man approached Casey. I had never met him before, and I thought I'd met all the staffers. He shuffled back and forth in his too-tight suit, making me think he'd been a few pounds lighter when he'd bought his clothes.

After a few words, he glanced in my direction and then back at Casey. He then pulled out a handkerchief from his pocket, dabbed his face, and left without a backward glance.

Whatever Casey said to him had scared the living shit out of him enough that he couldn't run away fast enough.

"Do I want to know what that was all about?" I asked, seeing a bit of agitation on Casey's face.

"President Kumar asked that you met him in his office." He gestured toward a hallway.

Once we cleared the additional security, I said, "It had to be more than just that."

"He broke procedure, and I informed him if he ever approached you without clearance that Mr. Kumar would hear about it."

I frowned. "If he dared to touch me, I could break every bone in his pudgy hand before he knew what hit him. Hell, you're the one who taught me the move."

"Yes, but no one is supposed to know this. As Secretary Camden said after the meeting, you will need to curb your reflexes. As far as anyone knows, you've spent the last few years taking on human rights cases that require hours in the courtroom, not time training to disarm combatants."

"I hope you're going to be available at god-awful hours to help me get out the aggression that's been building up without training."

"Give me the time and place, and I'll be there."

"I will hold you to that, and it may be sooner rather than later."

As I approached the closed doors of the office, two

Secret Service agents nodded their greetings and opened the door.

"Go right in, Ms. Zain."

I smiled and nearly ran straight into Senator Harrison from Georgia.

"Excuse me, Senator," I said, trying to steady myself.

He all but glowered at me. "You, young lady, are a terrible influence on him. With Kumar's approach to policy, I'd viewed him as a conservative in the guise of an independent. But now, with you in the picture, I'm not sure anymore."

"I believe you give me more credit than I deserve. Ashur is his own man and will do as he sees fit."

He snorted. "We'll see." Then he walked around me and into the hall.

The doors closed, making me jump.

Ashur held a tumbler in his hand and leaned against the wall near his desk, the Resolute Desk.

God. Could the man get any sexier?

He wore a dark gray suit custom made to fill out his very built six-three frame. His almost jet-black hair was cut short and combed neatly. Something I knew went against his natural style but was required as part of his job title. His light brown eyes stared at me in a way that made me think of things that were better left locked down.

This man was too good looking for his own good. No

wonder the press loved to comment about him being the "hot president."

A tingle shot into my core, and I felt the urge to shift my legs in hopes of curbing my need.

Why couldn't I get my hormones under control when I was around him? I wasn't the barely legal high school graduate anymore. Dammit, I was thirty-three fucking years old.

The slight curve to his lips told me he'd caught my reaction, but instead of saying anything, he offered me his tumbler. "Want a sip?"

I walked toward him, trying to ignore the cocky grin on his face, took the glass from his fingers, and brought it to my lips before taking a deep gulp of the scotch he preferred, a twenty-five-year-old Macallan.

The potent, over-the-top expensive liquid burned down my throat and gave me something to think about other than the desire I felt for the man next to me.

"What did Harrison say to you?" Ashur picked up a lock of my hair and twirled it around his callused finger.

"He thinks I'm a bad influence. And that my liberal views are rubbing off on you."

"He's just mad I sided with the Democrats on a pipeline he wants me to open up. He knew my stance on environmental issues even before the election. He'll get over it."

"Your nonchalance is going to get you in trouble. You

don't want the Republicans to close rank when you name your Supreme Court pick."

"I'll worry about that later. Like when Justice Bosworth announces her retirement."

I almost said she wasn't the only one planning to retire but kept my mouth shut. I'd have to disclose my source, and that would be open up a whole can of worms I wasn't ready to address.

After a few moments, he said, "You're good for me, Tara. You don't let me intimidate you, and you show me points of view that are opposite of mine."

"Now that is something I never expected to hear from your lips." I glanced at him, leaned a hip against a table by the window, and folded my arms. "You never give compliments twice in one day. What do you want from me?"

He came closer to me. "Now that's a loaded question."

He clasped the tumbler from my fingers, setting it on the windowsill.

Ashur's gaze perused my body.

"Like what you see, Mr. President?"

"Very much. Though I'd enjoy seeing what's under the designer outfit even more."

"Of course, you would," I responded a little too breathlessly.

And I'd like to lick down those six-pack abs you hide with those expensive suits you wear.

His hand glided along my arm and then settled on my hip.

My breath hitched, and the arousal I'd dulled with the alcohol reignited.

This would be so much easier if I wasn't crazy attracted to him. In the grand scheme of things, sexual desire for the man one would marry was a requirement. But this wasn't a normal relationship. It was a bargain wrapped in many strings.

I couldn't let my attraction cloud my judgment into forgetting this was business.

"Tara." Ashur's voice was gruff as he said my name.

"Yes."

"Sixty-one hours and you're mine."

The possessiveness in his statement made my stomach jump. And instead of annoyance at his claim on me, it aroused me.

"I know, Ashur."

"Ashu." His fingers flexed on my waist.

I licked my lips. "We're not lovers yet."

"You want me as much as I want you."

I gave a noncommittal hum but my pulse hammered in my ears.

He tilted my chin up with his index finger and leaned down, touching his forehead to mine. "Why have we waited so long? For two years, I've wanted nothing more than to get between those thighs of yours and make you scream my name as you came."

I'd thought of the same thing almost every day. I kept that tidbit to myself. Instead, I said, "You had your hand."

He lifted his head and peered into my eyes. "My palm is no comparison to your slick hot cunt rippling around my cock."

My throat dried up, and I swallowed. "Ash..." was all I got out before his mouth came down on mine.

The kiss started gentle, coaxing with soft passes of his lips, completely disarming me. The second I relaxed into the feel of him against me, he grew more demanding. I lost myself in a possessive, mind-blowing kiss. This definitely wasn't the gentle pecks he'd given me over the last year that had left me wanting, but a claiming, nothing held back, like a volcanic eruption of heat and desire.

How could I have forgotten how he kissed? My body was on fire, and I couldn't breathe. This man was too damn good at this.

If I didn't grab control of the situation, it could lead to trouble. But instead of pushing him away I met his demands with my own.

His tongue glided along mine in an intimate dance that made my nipples pebble into hard peaks inside the lace fabric of my bra. I clutched his arms, wanting to get closer to him.

He tasted of Macallen and orange, telling me he'd nibbled on the orange peel in his drink.

He lifted me onto the table, pushed the hem of my dress up and my legs wide, stepping between them. His thick, hard cock molded against my core.

A semblance of sanity hit, and I said, "We can't do this here." But then I threaded my fingers into his hair and deepened our embrace.

He sucked my lower lip into his mouth and then bit, making my core contract. "Why not? It's my office." His hands gripped my ass, grinding my clit along his length.

I gasped for air. "Because there are cameras everywhere and people could be watching."

"No one will see us—this is one of the spots in the room that doesn't have surveillance." He licked a line down my throat and then nipped my shoulder where it met the neck.

I moaned and arched to give him better access.

His fingers slid between my legs, and he pushed aside my underwear, rimming my soaked pussy.

I cried out, shifting my hips so he could stroke the spot I was desperate for him to touch. "Don't stop. Don't stop. Ashur please."

He pulled back, making me cry out in frustration.

"Not until you say it." He licked my essence from his fingers.

"Say what?" I whined.

"Say *Ashu*."

I stared into his amber depths, unable to utter a word. Why was it so important to call him by the silly nickname I'd given him when I was eighteen? Why did he need to hear it?

He touched my face with a gentle caress and then, ran a thumb across my lower lip. "You can say it, Tara. I am your lover. I will be the only lover you will have for the rest of your life."

I opened my mouth to retort but shut it when he lifted a brow daring me to deny his statement.

"Will I be your only lover?" I asked.

"Yes. I don't cheat. After you left, I can admit I played the field, but know this. I will never break the vows we made to each other."

The resolve in his voice made my heart ache.

"Ashur, don't say things like that. Or you'll have me believing what we have is more than a business arrangement."

A scowl crossed his face, and he stepped back. My words had broken the spell of the moment.

I slid off the table onto unsteady feet and tugged off my underwear. Thank God my dress was long and no one would know I'd gone commando.

As I reached for my purse, I noticed Ashur watching me. He'd straightened his clothes and now was back to the polished statesman.

He walked over to me, plucked my underwear from my hands, and then tucked it into his jacket pocket.

"Let's go entertain the 'rents."

"Are you really going into a family gathering with my thong in your pocket?"

"Yes."

"You're incorrigible."

"Never pretended otherwise." He smiled down at me, and my heart skipped a beat. There was a wicked glint in his eyes reminding me of the boy I'd known and not the too-straightforward-for-his-own-good president he was known for being.

He offered me his arm, and we walked out the door.

We stayed quiet, only greeting various staffers as we passed them.

By the time we took the stairs to the upper residence, my stomach was in knots, and any tingle of arousal from our office interlude had disappeared.

"Ashur?" I said as we took the hall leading to the Yellow Oval Room, where our parents waited.

"Yes?" We paused outside the doors.

"Are you sure you want to do this? We could announce we eloped and everyone would go home."

He looked down at me, tucked a stray hair behind my ear, and said, "Absolutely. You're the only woman I've ever considered marrying, and I can't wait for you to officially belong to me."

"It's about damn time the two of you showed up." The acid-laced words slapped us in the face the second the doors opened, washing the confusion I felt from Ashur's statement out in one swift blow.

God, I despised that man, father-in-law or not. He'd turned my life upside down. Because of him, my father had lost his job and had to move to a different state to find work. Because of him, I'd lost the one man who meant more to me than anything else on earth.

Yeah, I was officially marrying the very man in a few days, but it wasn't the way I'd dreamed it would have been. Instead of laughter and happiness, it was all business and end gains.

"Lord, help me not to kill him," I whispered, sending my wishful prayer up to heaven.

Ashur released a deep breath and responded, "You and me both."

"I mean it, Ashur. If he crosses the line, I won't hold back anymore."

"Go right ahead. After all, you are the first lady."

I shot him an annoyed glare, but he ignored me and moved into the room.

"Mummy," Ashur said, ignoring his father's curt words, and walked over to Anya Kumar, a beautiful Indian woman with soft golden skin and loving light brown eyes in the exact shade of her son's. He enveloped her in his large arms. "I missed you."

"You look tired, *betta*." She ran a thumb down his cheek. "This job is making you age."

"I'm fine. Don't worry so much."

"It is my job as your mummy."

I smiled at the love the two of them shared. For such a hard man, who'd spend a decade serving in the military, he was complete mush for his mom.

I couldn't blame him. I absolutely adored my future mother-in-law. She was everything and anything a girl could hope for in a mother-in-law: sweet, considerate, loving, and welcoming. It was the other half of the duo I dreaded seeing.

Ashur and Anya held each other for a moment longer and then Ashur stepped back and inclined his head to his father. "Papa."

A scowl crossed Minesh Kumar's face. "I left my business to attend your wedding." Then his gaze turned to me. "The least either of you could do is be here when we arrived."

I clenched my jaw. Yes, the President of the United States had nothing better to do than cater to his grumpy-ass father. And now my job as the first lady was to be at his beck and call.

Fuck that shit.

Minesh Kumar, technology billionaire and all-around elitist asshole viewed anyone who hadn't grown up in his social circle as beneath him. And, as the daughter of an ICU nurse and a lowly computer programmer in his empire, I was an ant to step on. He thought of me as an opportunistic gold digger and hadn't hidden his feelings.

He couldn't care less about all my degrees or that I was a world-renowned attorney who'd made a success of herself. All he saw was my pedigree.

Then there was the fact I ran an internationally successful law practice with his daughter, Samina Kumar-Camden. Never mind, that was a bad example.

He'd disowned Sam long ago. She'd chosen her own path in life and not the one her father had set out for her to follow. She'd become a celebrity attorney, joined forces with me to start our firm, married a conservative judge, and then decided to throw her hat into politics and became the junior senator from Washington State.

Most fathers would be overjoyed to have a child make a success of their careers, in politics or not. This wasn't the case for Minesh. He viewed it as a blow to his family name, more so now that both of his children had chosen a path in different realms than the one he envisioned them following.

I'd been Ashur's fiancée for over eighteen months and the man could barely look at me, much less welcome me as a future daughter-in-law.

I sighed and shrugged my shoulders. At least I had my parents. Anyone would have to be a moron not to like them.

Deciding to let Ashur deal with his father, I stepped around them and headed to the couch where my mom and dad stood.

"Daddy." Amir Zain picked me up and twirled me in a hug. "I'm so glad you made it safely."

"It is good to be here," he said as he set me on my feet.

My dad was a big, burly man with salt-and-pepper hair. I barely came up to his shoulder and in his arms, it always felt like home. Not a single day since the moment I could remember had he made me think I was anything less than amazing.

"I want a hug too." My mom stepped forward and wrapped her arms around me.

I kissed her cheek and soaked into her warmth and love.

It had been over three months since I'd last seen them. My parents had decided to do a world tour as a celebration of their mutual retirements.

They'd saved their whole life for their trip, and I couldn't blame them for having pride in achieving their goal or for extending it when they had the opportunity.

"You look well rested, Mummy."

Karina Zain was as gorgeous as always. Black hair that had only a sprinkling of gray and a figure that showed she took care of her health. "I swear you barely age."

She gave an unladylike "yeah right" snort, which made me laugh.

My family was real as they came. There was no pretension with them. They'd rather have people tell them what they really thought than put on a face. Maybe that was the reason my mother seemed to have an unending tank of tolerance for Minesh and his antics. Hell, his own wife could only take so much of his company before leaving a room.

"My glow is thanks to your soon-to-be husband. He extended our trip with a week in Tahiti. He offered us his private yacht to visit all the islands."

I turned a surprised glance at Ashur.

He shrugged. "Tara said it was your birthday. The ship was the least I could do."

A tinge of embarrassment colored his cheeks.

My goodness, the president was blushing.

The man kept surprising me.

I walked over to Ashur and whispered, "I promise not to tell a soul you're a sucker for our moms."

"You do that." He grazed his jaw across my forehead, sending goosebumps across my skin.

I pulled back, not wanting to linger, and I sat down with my parents on an antique yellow fabric couch.

After a few minutes of conversation, my mom took my hand in hers and said, "Ashur isn't the only one who looks tired. Are you okay? Samina called to check on us today and said you had to close your office."

"Mummy, I'm fine. My practice is still open. The junior partners are taking the lead now. Besides, the DC office was only a temporary location, so I could finish out a few cases before I assumed my duties as Ashur's wife."

She studied me for a second and then spoke in a hushed voice against my ear. "No more assignments, Tara. It's too dangerous."

"What?" I couldn't hide the surprise on my face.

She gave me her "I'm not as oblivious as you like to think" look she'd bestow on me when I was a kid and tried to sneak into the house after curfew.

All these years, I'd thought my parents had no idea about my life. Trust my mom to figure things out.

"I'm not sure what you're referring to, but if it makes you feel better, I'm all done until I'm in civilian life again."

I was saved from my mother's response by an interruption from Ashur's father.

"Why does Samina talk to you," Minesh asked, giving my mother a disgusted look, "but doesn't have the decency to call her own parents?"

"I'm sure Samina has contacted Anya. It isn't like her to be distant." My mother tried to defend Sam.

God where the hell was Sam? She had left Shawna's shop twenty minutes before I had, saying she wanted to pick up the kids so they could play interference between the grownups and the overgrown ass who'd provided half her DNA.

The only soft spot in Minesh Kumar's demeanor was Sam's kids. They were a handful but had a way of drawing even the stodgiest person into their antics. Samina may dislike her father but she'd never keep her children away from her mother. And therefore, because of Anya, Minesh was allowed time with the hellions.

"Don't make excuses for her. What could I expect from the likes of you?" Minesh Kumar came to stand in front of Mom and me.

I held my breath, trying to stifle a flippant response, but failed.

No one spoke to my mother this way.

I stood, refusing to let the asshole tower over me. I saw Ashur move from my peripheral vision and shook my head. It was my place to handle this.

"Don't ever disrespect my mother again. I've let you think less of me and talk down to my family and me for too long. I accepted it for the sake of Dad's job, and we know how well that turned out. Then it was for Ashur, but it ends now." I cocked a hand on my hip and stepped forward, making Minesh retreat. "Don't ever treat anyone I love like they're trash again. And let me make another thing clear in case your ego keeps you from seeing clearly. Samina has a relationship with me and my parents, where she doesn't have one with you. Did you actually expect the daughter you disowned and threw out of your house and refused to see to even consider contacting you? The only reason you're in this building is because of your wife."

The grooves on Minesh's face grew deeper and more pronounced. He turned to Ashur, pointing his finger at him. "Are you going to allow her to speak to me like this?"

"She hasn't said anything any of us haven't thought at least a hundred times in the last year." Ashur moved in my direction as a cold gleam entered his eyes.

Oh shit. That was the expression he got when he was about to take someone down with a few choice words. It was the look he'd gotten when his predecessor had questioned Ashur's military service during a presidential debate.

I'd better defuse Ash before the world learned what he really thought of his father.

When he was next to me, I took his hand in mine and whispered, "Thanks for having my back."

"We're a team." He ran a thumb along the skin on the outside of my hand. "Plus, I like watching you take charge, Commander."

Really? Was he calling me that in the middle of an argument with his father?

"Where is your loyalty, boy? I am still your father."

I opened my mouth to say something, but Ashur squeezed my fingers. "You had your say. Now it's my turn. I know how to handle him."

"Fine." I released an exasperated sigh. "Handle it your way. Just don't get any blood on the antique rugs."

"I'll do my best not to." He turned to Minesh but continued to hold my hand. "Papa, it is time to decide if you want to be part of our lives or not. Tara isn't going anywhere. She will be the mother of your grandchildren. If you ever want to see them, you better watch your tongue and actions. I learned how to be ruthless at your knee— don't think I won't use it against you."

The room grew completely silent with only the sound of the air conditioner blowing.

Holy fuck, Ashur had just threatened his father. Was I in a parallel universe?

"I see where I stand in this family." Minesh broke the quiet standoff between father and son.

"You do. Now—" Ashur tucked my arm in the crook of his elbow. "I believe it is time for dinner. Papa, you can join us or you can leave. The choice is yours."

With those words, Ashur led me out of a stunned room.

CHAPTER FIVE

Three hours after the most uncomfortable pre-wedding dinner on the face of the planet, I sat with my mom on a quiet bench in the rose garden of the White House.

"Are you sure you don't want to change your mind and start drinking?" I joked to my mom.

"That man could drive a person to do it, but I have more resolve than that. Plus, I wouldn't give him the satisfaction."

After Ashur's statement, the evening was anything but pleasant. Minesh spent the dinner complaining about everything from the food to the uncomfortable chairs to the stuffiness of the old building. The only saving grace was when Samina and Devin arrived with their two children, DJ and Mira. The toddlers were so full of life, asking questions and requesting kisses that even the asshole cracked a smile.

However, the moment dinner ended, my mother and I escaped to the gardens, Anya and Samina left for Sam's townhouse to put the kids to bed, and the men...well, I wasn't sure where they'd gone. Mummy and I wanted out of the Residence so badly that we barely said our goodbyes.

My phone rang with a tone that made my stomach hurt. This was not good.

I was no longer part of this world, so why were calls still forwarded to me?

I glanced around, opened my purse, and then pulled out the mobile, scanning the caller ID.

My heartbeat accelerated.

It was Ameera's mobile, but I knew it couldn't be her.

God, I hoped Tyler was monitoring this call.

"Hello," I answered, trying not to fidget as my mother scrutinized me.

"Where is my daughter?" Hamir Ustaf's deep, agitated voice said in Urdu, a language native to the area around North India and Pakistan.

I'd grown up speaking the two languages of my parents. My father's being Urdu and my mother's being Gujarati, a language spoken in the Gujarat region of India. My parents had been the scandal of their age.

They'd met while studying abroad in the United States at the University of Texas. As my mom liked to tell me, one look from across their university classroom and she knew her destiny was sealed.

I'd had the same reaction to Ashur when I'd walked down the hallway of Kumar Technologies for a lunch date with my father.

I shook the thought from my mind and focused on the dipshit on the phone.

"Who is this?" I responded in English, knowing it would annoy the shit out of Hamir.

"Don't fuck with me. That girl is my property. She was supposed to come to me, but because of you, they kept her. And now there is a third bidder."

My hand shook with anger. I knew if I were standing I'd have swayed. This bastard had arranged for Ameera's kidnapping. How had our intelligence team missed this? The agents who constantly watched him hadn't picked up an inkling of news he'd been involved in the abduction.

I kept my voice cool as I said, "She is no one's property."

"My daughter, my property."

"Sperm donor doesn't make you a father. You abandoned her mother for a lucrative marriage in another country. Do your wife or heirs know you have an illegitimate child with an American model?"

"Because of you, her cost has tripled."

"I'm not the one who expected a terrorist group to play fair when he had his biological daughter kidnapped. Did you really think I wouldn't do everything I could to find her?"

"Drop out of the auction or I will make your life a living hell. How do you think your husband will feel when he learns your secret activities?"

"What makes you think he doesn't know?" I glanced at my watch and then clenched my fists.

Twenty more seconds and we'd have a trace in addition to the recording of this conversation.

If I went with my first instinct, the second his location was established I'd send in the most overzealous team in Solon to get rid of the bastard immediately.

But it would cause more grief than I needed and the priority was getting Ameera back, not starting a war.

My mother set a hand on my arm, making me jump, and then glared at me.

"I'm not an idiot. A man like Kumar would never let his woman interfere in affairs that aren't her concern."

"Some men are more secure in their manhood than others. If you really think I'll let Ameera go from one living hell to another, you have another think coming."

"As I said, don't go against me or you will be in the middle of a scandal that will ruin any chance of your husband winning reelection."

The line went dead, and a sense of anxiety hit me.

God, please keep Ameera alive until we can get her out.

I sent my prayer to heaven, stood, and turned to my mother.

"I'm sorry, Mummy. I need to make another call."

She frowned and then nodded.

I dialed Tyler's number. The second he came on the line, I said, "Tell me you got the trace."

"No. Only the recording."

My heart sank. I knew it was too good to be true. I hoped luck would throw us a bone and a trace would lead us directly to Hamir but it wasn't in the cards.

"Any luck with your leads on locating the package?"

"Nothing yet but I'm following a few leads."

I pushed down the disappointment. "Tyler, she's been missing too long."

"You think I don't know this?"

"I'm sorry. I'm worried."

"Forget about it. Just make sure the money goes into the account by the end of this coming week."

"Already scheduled."

"Tara, you didn't have to marry Ash for his money. He would have given it to you regardless of whether you married him."

I winced. "That's not the only reason for this."

"I know the reason. Do you?"

"Leave it alone."

"I can't do that. I wouldn't be a friend otherwise. You know Ameera would agree. We've kept each other accountable for years. I won't stop just because she isn't here."

"I can't right now, Ty. Let it go."

"Fine. I'll see you tomorrow when I transition to my groomsmen's duties." He hung up.

I took a deep breath and returned my attention to my mother. There was no hiding my agitation from her, and I was pretty sure she'd caught some of my conversation with Hamir.

The best course of action was to pretend all was good and hope she believed me.

"Where were we?"

Mummy frowned, looked around, and then said in Gujarati, *"No more adventures. You hear me."*

I was in deep shit.

"Yes. I hear you," I responded in Gujarati.

"I want a few answers, and then I won't ever ask about it again."

I sighed and then nodded. *"Go ahead."*

"How long have you been doing this other job?"

"I can't tell you."

"When did you stop practicing law?"

"I never stopped, Mummy."

"How did you get that scar on your shoulder?"

"I fell." How was I going to say someone tried to punch me, and when I tried to avoid the blow, I tumbled into a shelf?

"Are you going to give me a straight answer to any of my questions?"

"I am giving you the information I can."

Mummy growled and folded her arms across her chest. Oh shit. She was pissed.

"Are you planning to have children?"

"Yes. Within the next two years." It was a condition of the contract, but I kept that information to myself.

"Tara, I will never forgive you if you leave any children you have without a mother. You are done with this life that makes it necessary to have a gun on you at all times. Am I making myself clear?"

Well hell. She knew about the piece I tended to carry the majority of the time.

"Yes, Mummy."

"Does Ashur know?"

"That I carry a gun? Probably not."

That was the wrong thing to say because her eyes grew angry. She opened her mouth to give me a piece of her mind but shut it as she caught sight of Ashur coming outside with my father and Devin. At least Minesh wasn't with them. Thank God for small favors.

"We will continue this discussion later."

"Yes, Mummy."

I had no fear she would say anything to anyone. My mother would step in front of a bullet before putting my life in danger or causing me any more scandals than the ones I tended to put myself in.

Mummy stood and said in English, "Did you come to enjoy this beautiful summer night with us?"

"A man had to be insane not to want an evening with the two beautiful women he loves," my dad stated. "Wouldn't you agree?"

"Absolutely," Ashur said as he watched me with a predatory gaze.

He took my hand in his and pulled me to my feet. A wave of need pulsed to life, and the anxiety of my conversations with Tyler and Mummy disappeared from my mind.

I wanted this man with a desperation I'd never felt for anyone else.

"I'm counting the seconds, Tara."

My heart skipped a beat, and I licked my now dry lips, knowing without a doubt that I was in deep trouble...and not because of my secrets.

CHAPTER SIX

I stirred as rough stubble grazed up my inner thighs. My body was on fire, covered in sweat and in need of release.

I moaned, "More. Please more."

Gripping thick, wavy hair, I tried to position the mouth delving into my core to the spot I was desperate for touch.

"I'll stop if you don't move those hands back into position." He lifted his head and stared up my body to my face.

"You're making me crazy." I glowered at him but threw my head back as he swiped a tongue down the length of my lower lips.

"Then you know how I've felt for the past two years. You made us wait, knowing how explosive we are in bed."

Lifting my hips, I rode the fingers he'd pressed into my sopping core.

"Oh God. Ashu, I'm almost there."

"I know, baby."

"Then why won't you let me come?"

He stopped his ministrations and slid up my body, letting his hard cock glide into the folds of my sex.

My pussy spasmed, readying itself for his invasion.

"Because you have to come to me. I told you I'd stick to our bargain. The only person who can break the no-sex-until-marriage rule you asked for is you." He pressed in a fraction and then retreated.

"So, you're going to leave me hanging?"

"That is your decision." He laughed and thrust deep.

I cried out, sitting straight up in bed, and gasped for air. I searched the dark room for Ashur.

Son of a bitch. It was another one of those tormenting dreams.

Every day for the last week, I'd dreamed of Ashur and me in some sexual situation or another.

What had happened in Ashur's office yesterday was only adding to the frustration I felt.

I'd tried self-gratification, but it left me unsatisfied. What was the point of my battery-operated boyfriend if I couldn't get the relief I wanted?

I threw myself down onto my mattress and wiped a hand down my sweat-covered face.

Turning, I glanced at the clock.

Four AM. Fuck.

This was getting ridiculous.

Maybe my dreams were getting worse because of the fact Ashur had become more forward the closer we got to the wedding. Or maybe it was because I'd gone years without needing sex and my body was ready to break free from the self-imposed drought.

I rolled over onto my stomach and covered my head with my pillow. How the hell was I going to go back to sleep when my body ached for a man I shouldn't want to this level?

You'll crave me as much as I crave you.

Ashur had said those words to me, not knowing that my desire for him hadn't stopped in the past fifteen years.

Shit, I had to get some rest, but I'd only be wasting time lying in bed for the next two hours.

Maybe I could get Casey up for a sparring match in the basement. He'd probably bitch, but he had offered.

Besides, even if I decided to go for a run, he'd have to go with me. So, a workout in my townhouse was the better alternative.

I reached over and grabbed my cell phone and dialed his number.

"Stop dawdling and hit me," Casey yelled as he

knocked me on my ass for the fourth time in less than twenty minutes.

"I hate you," I muttered.

I'd thought getting Casey up for sparring match was a good idea, but now I was rethinking my stupidity. My fifth-degree black belt skills meant nothing against his seventh. Especially when I hadn't trained properly in over a year and a half.

Casey was killing me, and from the look on his face, he loved it.

Bastard.

When I'd first met Casey, he'd been one of my training instructors in Solon. His job had been to weed out anyone who couldn't cut it as part of the organization. By the end of the eight-week course, I'd called Casey every name in the book and believed he was the spawn of Satan, but I'd made it to the next level. I hadn't realized it at the time, that Casey was hardest on those he saw potential. And to this day I am forever grateful he taught me ways to use my petite, five-foot-two size as an asset.

He'd remained a mentor until I'd started taking assignments and moved up in the chain of command. Then, he'd become a friend. I'd known it was more than a coincidence that he was now the lead in my Secret Service detail. The man had connections and a way of maneuvering bureaucratic red tape that could boggle the mind. Casey viewed me as the daughter he'd never had and wouldn't let anyone else head my protection.

No one outside of Solon knew of my connection to Casey beyond his current position. In the public eye, we'd kept a professional relationship. It was only in situations like this one, where we were trying to beat the shit out of each other at four forty-five in the morning that we let our guard down.

I rested my head on the concrete floor, gasped in shallow breaths, and then glared at Casey. "I'm exhausted, dammit."

His bright green eyes crinkled at the corners and his lips turned up in amusement. "I'm not the masochist who wanted an MMA workout the day before her wedding."

"You're my security. You're supposed to talk me out of stupid decisions." I grimaced as I struggled to stand. "If I have bruises, Neya is never going to forgive me."

"When the wife to my new boss wakes me at a god-awful hour and asks to work out, I give her what she wants. Plus, you have something more to worry about than Neya."

I frowned and took the proper stance. "Like what?"

"How you're going to explain the bruises to your soon-to-be husband. If I hadn't pulled back in time, you'd have a nice black and blue shoulder accessory to go with your sleeveless wedding lengha. That man notices everything about you, if you haven't realized."

I straightened. I hadn't thought about that. In less than

twenty-four hours we'd be married and on our way to our honeymoon. And I was already going to have to explain a few of my older scars. It would be better not to add a new one to the list.

"Shit. That puts a damper on any more sparring." I released a deep breath. "You're mean whenever anyone wakes you early and more than likely will continue this beat-down if I don't end this now."

"Excellent observation, Commander."

"Not you too with the Commander shit. Really? Tyler put you up to it, didn't he?"

Casey's lips turned up a bit before he went back to his usual serious expression. "Secretary Camden is too busy of a man to discuss ways to annoy you."

I walked over to a bin of towels and picked up two, throwing one to Casey.

"Yes, Mr. I'm-a-Prankster would never put you up to anything. Especially not something that gets me riled up."

"It is who you are."

I rolled my eyes and decided to change the subject. "I let you knock me around for the last half-hour to help me release aggression not antagonize me. Now, I'm back to square one."

Casey wiped his face. "You could sneak into your fiancé's bedroom and take it out on him. I'm sure he'd be more than happy to accommodate you."

"Not funny. I thought you were on my side."

"I've been on your side since the moment you walked through the doors of that training facility in Geneva."

I remembered that day like it was yesterday. It was the summer before I started law school. My former professors at Harvard had offered me an internship with an "international relief organization," saying it was the perfect stepping stone for my future career in international law. Needless to say, I'd learned more than I'd bargained for or expected and entered a world I hadn't known existed.

I wiped the perspiration on the back of my neck and held the towel to my face. "I know."

"Now back to the subject you wanted to change. Your man wants you. You want your man. The least you could do is reduce the tension everyone feels whenever the two of you are in the same room."

"What's that supposed to mean?" I threw the towel to the ground, grabbed my water bottle, and then gulped down the cool liquid.

"You are the furthest thing from traditional. What are you waiting for?"

"First Samina and now you. Does everyone know I'm not fucking Ashur?" I ran a hand over my heated face.

"I'm your security."

I frowned, picked up my towel, and threw it at him. "That's your answer?"

"It's a better answer than anything you're giving me." He stood, going over to the corner where his gym bag was and pulling out a jacket. "Besides, I know the answer. I just want to see if you'll admit it."

I crossed my arms across my body. "Oh, wise one, please tell me what is my reason for not sleeping with my fiancé?"

He walked toward the stairs that led to the kitchen. He set a foot on the bottom step, stared me in the eyes, and smiled. "Because you're in love with him and you're worried he'll break your heart again once he learns all your secrets."

CHAPTER SEVEN

After a long shower and a giant cup of coffee, I found myself working in the home office of my townhouse.

I'd tried my damnedest to focus on the list of tasks I had to complete, but Casey's words kept haunting me and left me in a foul mood.

In love with Ashur, as if.

Ashur and I had become friends over the last year and a half, moving past the anger and heartache of our youth. However, that didn't mean I was in love with him. And our mutual attraction only indicated that we'd have mind-blowing sex. Nothing more.

I was not in love. I knew better than to fall down that rabbit hole.

I glanced at my ring and sighed.

Who was I kidding? I was fucked. And not just literally. Great, now I was thinking about the dream.

I groaned and pressed my fingertips to my temples.

"Ms. Zain. Your gown has arrived, and the designer wants to make sure it fits."

I turned my office chair toward my assistant, Eleanor, or Eli as I called her.

She was a slender woman in her late forties with long blond hair and gray eyes. I'd hired her as my assistant eight years ago, right after her husband, a former Solon agent, had died from a heart attack. As a new widow, she was looking for a complete change of career from teaching theater at the University of Washington. Eli understood the lifestyle I lived, having experienced decades of it as an agent's wife. She also accepted the complexity of managing a public career and having another very secret one.

I'm not sure what I would have done without her. She had a way of keeping me in check, and sometimes I wondered if she knew more about my job than I did.

Thank God she'd agreed to move across the country with me. She was the presence I needed to keep me grounded in this intimidating world I now existed in.

"What gown?"

She typed away on her tablet with a distinct frown on her face. "The one for your first official dinner as the first lady."

"Oh, God." I dropped my head onto the desk. "I totally forgot about the fitting."

The last thing I needed to focus on was a state dinner planned for the week Ashur and I returned from our honeymoon.

I had to get these last-minute tasks completed for my law practice, make sure Tyler was set for as smooth a transition as possible, and double check the details of Ameera's auction and hopeful rescue. And then there was the fact my body hurt like hell from the beat-down Casey had given me at my insistence. If the pain I felt in my hip was any indication, I'd have a bruise. Shit, now I'd have to explain the mark as Casey predicted I would.

What the hell had I been thinking?

That you needed a distraction from thoughts of jumping the man you're marrying but shouldn't want so desperately.

"Can we reschedule? I have too much to do. Plus, I have to get to the last-minute wedding logistics meeting before the rehearsal."

"No. The designer is here, and it's better to get it over with. The meeting isn't for two hours, giving you plenty of time have the fitting and finish up your work."

I wasn't going to win this one. No one got between Eli and her agenda.

"Fine. Have them set up in the guest bedroom. It's the only room not filled with boxes."

She nodded, stepped out of the room, giving Casey instructions, and then returned in less than two minutes.

"Please tell me you aren't wearing red to your first official gala as first lady."

"It was the only thing that looked great on my body and didn't cost an arm and a leg."

"You do realize you're marrying a billionaire? He can afford a high-end gown."

That was something I didn't need a reminder of. I was going to use Ashur's money for more important things. Like freeing Ameera.

"It wouldn't look appropriate if I wore custom-made haute couture clothing. I won't have anyone question Ashur's fiscally conservative stance. Now to respond to the red dress comment. The gown was Jacinta's and Samina's idea. They wanted me to distinguish myself from past First Ladies. Since I agreed with them, I chose a dress that suited my personality."

She cocked a hand on her hip and glared at me. "I see your point on the cost and keeping your personal style, but red? Really?"

"Really," I retorted and then signed a few last-minute account transfers documents Tyler needed. "I like red. I look good in it. End of story."

"I know when it's a lost cause." She used her stylus to check off something on the tablet.

"You know if you keep scowling, your face is going to freeze that way," I said with a smirk.

Eli could give Attila the Hun a run for his money when it came to annoyed glares.

"I'm charged with keeping your life organized. If you don't have it together, then it's my fault."

"You take your job too seriously."

"I'm supposed to. There is a huge difference between being your PA in Seattle and managing the first lady's schedule."

"I have complete faith in your ability to coordinate my life. You'll do a much better job than I ever would."

Eli approached me and then took a seat across from me. Uh-oh, I shouldn't have said that. Eli may work for me, but she was like a no-nonsense aunt who told it like it was, whether I wanted to hear it or not.

I pushed back from my chair and folded my arms across my body. "Let me have it. You've got something on your mind."

"Are you truly going to give up everything you've built in your practice and Solon to become first lady?"

The last thing I wanted to do was give up the jobs that had given me my identity for all of my adult life, but what choice did I have? I also wanted a child, and I'd never ever put my child knowingly in danger, despite what Mummy believed.

Yes, two children were part of the agreement, but I

hadn't hesitated when Ashur put babies as part of our arrangement. I'd wanted to be a mother but had resigned myself for it never to happen. This was the reason I'd immersed myself in Solon so much that I'd surpassed other agents in rank who'd been at the organization longer. Now that parenting was part of my future, I'd settle for a life I never expected to have happy and healthy kids.

"You know as well as I do that flying all over the world for all my causes isn't possible anymore."

"But will you be happy in this new role?"

"I don't know, Eli." I sighed. "All I can hope for is that I find a project that can keep my focus without being a liability for Ashur. I'm not polished or sophisticated or well-groomed for the role I'm in. The one project I could have gotten involved in I gave to my predecessor and she's gone global with the endeavor."

A little over three years ago, I had been part of a Solon operation focused on stopping an underground ring specializing in the sale of child brides on US soil. This group targeted poor immigrant families from the Middle East and Asia, who were struggling financially and barely living above the poverty line. These parents sold their daughters to wealthy men who were looking for a legal way into the United States. The girls had no choice in what happened to them, and if they refused, they were either thrown out of their homes or physically harmed. These parents viewed the dowry earned more than worth giving up a child to a man who could be five times their age.

My team had flown to Pakistan where some of the girls were being held and bartered for their safe release. I knew when I'd gone in that the men I was meeting with were on the US terror watch list, but my priority had been to free the seventy-plus American girls being held until their "fiancés" could come to get them. I'd negotiated their release, but an American conservative reporter had recognized me from my international casework, taken pictures, and then written a piece about me. It had caused a national stir, and President Edgar had made it his mission to make an example of me. He hadn't cared that I'd fought to bring back American citizens who were being held in captivity; it had only mattered that he could make an example of me and use it as a platform to campaign for reelection.

Thankfully, Jacinta and Samina had come to my rescue. They'd introduced me to First Lady Amanda Edgar, who was looking for something that distinguished herself from her inflammatory husband and together we created the No Bride Initiative, focused on stopping the epidemic of child brides in America. I never expected Mrs. Edgar to have such a passion for the work, but she had, and now it had become an international organization. And thus, I was left without something that I could grab onto as my lifeline in the political world I would never belong.

"You don't have to fit into the roles other first ladies took on. You can be yourself."

I gave her my "are you kidding me?" look.

"Listen to what I have to say before you tune me out."

"Fine. Go ahead."

"You can still be part of Solon, just not in the field. Nearly all past directors took hands-off behind-the-scenes roles. You're the only one who has ever taken active field assignments after climbing the ranks."

"So, you think I can do my first lady duties, have lots of little Kumar babies, and run operations for Solon?"

"Without a doubt. You ran a successful law practice with crazy, high-profile clients, took on pro-bono cases that made international headlines, and had an additional over-the-top demanding career without cracking."

Well, when she put it that way, why not add a couple of kids, political jockeying, and a sexy-as-sin president to the mix?

Not! Taking all of that on would write me a first-class ticket to Looneyville.

"I think you give me too much credit."

"I'm only telling you how I see it."

"It's too late, even if I wanted to change my mind. I had my resignation meeting two months ago when I joined Ashur on his presidential tour of Europe."

She set her tablet in front of me and pointed at the document she'd pulled from our secure cloud. "According to your contract, you can rescind any resignation within six months of notification."

"And how would you know this?"

She lifted a brow. "I read everything that passes over my desk."

"And?" I folded my arms across my body.

"And today I received a special courier delivery with a rebuttal letter from the board saying they will wait six months before making your resignation official, per your contract. This means you can still change your mind."

I released a sigh. "You're like a pit bull with a bone. Fine. I'll think about it."

"That's all I ask." She checked her watch. "Now, time for the fitting you're determined to avoid."

I frowned, moved from around my desk, and headed to meet the designer of my gown.

CHAPTER EIGHT

Around ten thirty, I wrapped up the fitting and any remaining paperwork. This left me with enough time to get to the Executive Residence before the pre-wedding briefing. It almost sounded ridiculous to have such precautions for a wedding, but then I wasn't marrying a regular man and the security needed for the media frenzy was twice as intense as it had been for Ashur's inauguration day.

Samina and Jacinta were used to the spotlight of the camera, but the rest of the wedding party wasn't, and I wanted to make sure they understood all the precautions we'd put in place. Everyone who was part of the wedding, from the parents and friends to extended family, would stay at the Invictus, a hotel owned by one of Jacinta's close friends, Kevin Stanton. He'd literally shut down the entire building to house the wedding party and increased security so much that Ashur had joked it was more protected than Fort Knox. The only people not staying at the hotel were the invited international dignitaries. They caused a security nightmare that required their own hotel and team.

"Good morning, First Lady," came a voice to my left as I entered the main hall.

A middle-aged woman with salt-and-pepper hair and one of the sweetest demeanors I'd ever encountered smiled at me. She was one of the morning housekeepers who kept everything dust free and sparkling. She had worked for the last three administrations and knew all the ins and outs of the building. She could have retired years ago, but she enjoyed her position and as she'd told me not so long ago, she refused to let some know-it-all take her job and change things.

"I'm not first lady yet, Eleanor."

"In less than twenty-four hours you will be, and then you can redecorate this place with your own sense of style." Eleanor turned her nose up at a few antique figurines near her, and I couldn't help but laugh.

I could always use a dose of Eleanor to cheer me up. Too bad my decorating sense was lacking. I wasn't sure she'd approve of anything I'd pick. Now show me some designer clothing or an arsenal of handguns, and I was the girl for the job.

"I'll make sure to consult you before deciding on

anything. You would know better than anyone what this place needs to liven it up. Does that sound like a plan?"

Her eyes lit up. "I would love that."

"Ms. Zain, this way. Your family is waiting for you in the Yellow Oval Room to go over the final details of the wedding." Casey directed me up a flight of stairs leading to the second floor.

The moment I stepped onto the landing, I saw Veer George, Ashur's vice-president and Jacinta's husband. He was as handsome as Ashur but with a sexy pirate-ish edge, probably due to the scar that ran down his right cheek. He wore his jet-black hair a bit longer than one expected a politician to have, which added to his rakish appearance.

Recently a celebrity magazine voted him the "sexiest man of the year." He'd hated that title, but Jacinta loved it. Who didn't want a husband who was hot as sin and totally into her?

As Jacinta would say, she was one lucky bitch.

Veer's hazel eyes were filled with amusement the second I came into view.

"Where are you off to?" I asked, since he was the best man and was supposed to be in the meeting with the wedding party.

"I've got to make a quick call. Then I'll join you in the Yellow Oval Room."

I shook my head. "Is Papa-in-law in there?"

"Yep. As is the whole wedding party."

"Sam decided on the room, didn't she?"

"Does that question really need an answer?"

"I guess not." I laughed.

Samina knew her father hated the color yellow and therefore that was the room everyone would use whenever Minesh Kumar was around.

It was Sam's passive-aggressive way of annoying the shit out of her father. And if I was honest about it, I loved her sick sense of vengeance.

"I better stop dawdling and head in there."

"Subtle has never worked with him. Just be straightforward," Veer said with a gleam in his eye.

"Should I assume that you heard about our family dinner?"

"Possibly. All I can say is that it was about time." Veer kissed my cheek and headed down the hall.

"Let's go, Casey. Hopefully, Ashur won't be too long."

As I took the corner, an unexpected level of worry rolled into the pit of my stomach. I covered my abdomen with my palm and tried to push back the uneasiness.

Tomorrow, I'd live here. In this palatial home as the first lady.

Gone was the daughter of the no-name technology programmer and nurse, gone was the human rights attorney, and definitely gone was the North American director of Solon.

It had killed me not to strap my thigh piece on today,

but my mother had ordered me not to have it on me at any time during the wedding. We'd never finished our garden conversation but I'd gotten the gist of her message. She was right—I couldn't risk my future for the life I'd agreed to step away from.

Just as I approached the doors to the Yellow Oval Room, Leara Crawford, Ashur's personal secretary, approached me.

She wore a tailored gray suit, with a fire-engine red blouse underneath and matching Louboutin heels. At near seventy, Leara was stylish in the way women dreamed of being at any age. I so wanted to be her when I grew up.

"Hi, Leara."

"Ms. Zain," she responded, making me frown. It still took me a second to get used to how people formally addressed me, especially when I'd known them outside of the political world.

Before joining Ashur's team, Leara had been a policy research specialist at the United Nations. She was my go-to expert for various cases. And because of her, I was able to navigate countless situations that required an in-depth knowledge of laws in non-US-friendly countries.

"Do I want to know what's going on in there?"

A smile touched Leara's lips. "There is a level of frost growing on the light fixtures that makes me think you'll need a jacket to ward off the chill."

"So, no friendly conversations and excitement for the

wedding?" I asked, knowing anything in that realm of that line of thinking was a long shot when Minesh Kumar was in the vicinity.

She shook her head in response.

Leara had been privy to Minesh Kumar's explosion of anger when he'd learned I was the one Ashur had asked to marry. The man had refused to accept the engagement and went as far as to tell Ashur he'd disown him for marrying filth like me and to threaten that I'd lose my fancy career with the right words from him.

It had taken all my strength not to punch him. The man thought he could use the same tactics he'd used on the girl who had to choose between the boy she loved and her father's career and livelihood.

To my surprise, Ashur had stepped in as he'd done the other day and asked his father to leave if he couldn't show me respect.

"Senator Kumar-Camden has been playing interference by having the children in the room, but I think she has reached her limit for her father's antics."

"Got to love Sam for trying. What about Jacinta? Minesh loves her, and she can usually occupy his time with discussion about Texas business for hours."

Leara winced. "I believe Senator Camden-George is no longer his favorite after she told him not to talk down to Senator Kumar-Camden or question her parenting."

"Jacinta's pregnancy has caused her to lose her

tolerance for drama. Let me go in and focus his wrath on me. I'm a tough gal. I can handle it." I squared my shoulders and prepared myself for the meeting.

"I know you can, but that isn't why I'm here. President Kumar wants a word with you in private."

"About?" I asked, not understanding why my heartbeat jumped a notch as I thought about being alone in a room with Ashur.

It wasn't as if we hadn't spent time by ourselves before. It had been a weekly occurrence since Ashur had taken office. It was during those evenings that our friendship had grown. We'd discuss everything from pop culture to politics and our various stances on everything and anything, many times us being on opposite sides. However, until two days ago, we'd never crossed the line to anything physical, even with the undercurrent of desire constantly lingering between us. Now that we'd knocked down the wall I'd erected, there was no stopping either of us from acting on our attraction.

A tingle went up my spine and a pulse of desire began a steady throb between my legs.

"Where should I meet him? His office?" I glanced at Casey, who stepped back from the Yellow Oval Room doors.

Leara shook her head. "In the master suite."

I licked my lips and then swallowed.

What was the man up to?

I'd never spent any time in the master bedroom. Even when the movers brought my things in, my assistant had supervised.

I wasn't the naive eighteen-year-old who believed in happily ever after, and Ashur wasn't the up-and-coming college graduate who viewed me as the most precious person in his life. This time, there wasn't any expectation other than what was stated in the contract. We both knew where we stood on things, especially the past. This was a business arrangement, nothing more.

Now, if only my heart could remember this.

At least I'd have the children I'd always wanted. Even though this wasn't the way I'd planned to have them.

"He said you don't have to knock and to go right in. He wants to greet everyone together."

I nodded and walked down the hall, pausing for a brief moment before I entered the bedroom.

The first thing I noticed was the elegant simplicity of the space. It possessed little of the over-the-top old-world glamour of Ashur's predecessor. The colors were a combination of light tones of creams, whites, and grays mixed with furnishings that were stylish and usable.

There was the scent of spiced cologne and soap in the air, telling me Ashur was in the shower.

My pulse jumped and need flared to life in my core.

I walked over to the seer curtain-covered windows, setting my purse on a nearby table. Tucking my loose hair behind my ear, I pulled back the drapes and gazed out at the breathtaking view of the manicured lawn.

Never in a million years would I have believed Ashur Kumar, the boy whose heart I'd broken when we were barely out of our youth, would want to marry me almost fifteen years later, much less want to have children with me.

And even more unfathomable was that me, Tara Rayna Zain, controversial human rights attorney, was about to become first lady.

At that moment, the door leading out of the bathroom opened and a whiff of steam billowed into the room.

"You could have joined me, Tara. It isn't as if you haven't seen the goods before."

CHAPTER NINE

I turned to face Ashur and came to an abrupt halt.

Instead of the impeccably tailored suit I expected him to be in, he wore a large towel wrapped around his waist. He rubbed his damp hair with a small cloth as beads of water trailed along the tanned skin of his broad shoulders and washboard abs.

It took all my effort not to lick my lips.

His honed form was a work of art.

He no longer possessed the lean physique of the boy I'd fallen in love with but that of a man who'd built his muscles from years of military training. There wasn't an inch of unnecessary fat on him, and his chiseled abs would put a bodybuilder to shame. The only things marring his gorgeous form were the slight scars on his waist and chest. He'd incorporated them into the Indian-inspired tattoos that covered most of the left half of his upper body, making me want to trace each design around them. Not just with my finger but my tongue.

And then there was the way the towel clung to him. Dear lord, a woman had to be dead not to drool and hope for a peek at the package hidden under the cloth.

Shit, what was I doing?

Get your hormones in check, Tara Zain. Your entire family is waiting for you down the hall.

I ignored my self-reprimand and continued to examine Ashur's body. Politicians were supposed to be balding with potbellies. Not sexy as sin, covered in tattoos, and looking like they should be on the cover of a wet Wednesday calendar.

"Want me to lose the towel?" A smirk touched his lips.

Damn. He'd caught me staring at his body.

"I'll let you touch me anywhere you desire. I only ask that I get to return the favor."

I crossed my arms and tapped my foot and desperately hoped he hadn't caught the heat on my cheeks or the pebbling of my nipples.

"Why are you taking a shower now?"

"Tyler and I went for a run."

"I didn't know you were still training for the marathon."

He wiped the stray water from his hair. "I'm not, but I needed something to take the edge off and a long, hard run is only a small consolation for what I really want."

His gaze bored into mine as a wave of heavy lust flooded my system.

"Will you get dressed? Our wedding party is waiting for us." I gave him my most no-nonsense voice, the one that I used during negotiations. "Samina is probably on the verge of stabbing your father at any moment."

"Are you sure you want me to put on clothes? The way your body reacts every time I'm near tells me otherwise."

"It tells you nothing." I was such a liar. He knew it. I knew it.

If I didn't want him, I wouldn't have nearly let him take me in his office, against an antique side table, in the only spot a camera couldn't record us.

The memory added to my desire and I barely held in a moan.

He walked toward me with a predatory gleam in his eyes that made me want to retreat.

"Oh, but it does. Want me to list the ways?"

I lifted my chin and challenged, "Go ahead."

Why the hell did I say that?

He took a step. "I'll start with the way your breath changes when my hand grazes your lower back as we walk into any room together."

Step.

"Then there is the flush that tinges your skin as you watch me and think about how I'd fucked you if you hadn't imposed the no-sex rule."

Step.

"Then the most telling sign is how you unconsciously press your thighs together whenever I'm near you."

Oh hell, he'd caught that.

"I think the 'hot president' title has gotten to your head."

My back hit the wall, and one of his arms braced against my side.

"The only thing that has gotten to my head is you." He grabbed my hand and pressed it against his growing cock.

I jerked as if the fire had burned me, but Ashur kept my palm pressed against him.

"I've spent the last two years thinking about the many ways I planned to fuck you. Our sex life was fantastic in the past, and I know it will be even more scorching now."

"Then one more day shouldn't be a burden," I said in a breathless whisper.

"I don't think you have any idea what it's like to see your clothes moved into our closet and not have you here. I want to feel you under me, over me, and everything in between. I want the game we're playing to end."

"Ashur, please."

"Do you really want to wait?"

"Yes," I gasped, trying to resist the urge to wrap my fingers around him and failing as I began to stroke his firm, terry-covered erection.

A pleasure-filled groan came from him, and he

dropped his forehead against mine. "Then I suggest you stop. I don't have the will or the inclination to do it."

I should put an end to this madness. We were due to see our parents at any moment. But he felt so good in my hand. I'd forgotten how thick and long he was. I twisted my wrist, gliding up to the flared head of his cock, and squeezed.

"Harder, Tara. Harder."

I released my hold on him long enough to yank his towel free, and then gripped him again, pumping my fist up and down. The velvet heat of him made me want to drop to my knees and engulf him in my mouth.

"No. That is not where I want your mouth right now. The taste I had of you in my office has consumed my mind, keeping me from clearly thinking about anything else." His fingers threaded into my hair, pulling my head back, and he covered my lips with his.

At first, his kiss was gentle, and then it moved to demanding. With a snap, all the need and pent-up desire I'd reined in with my workout erupted. He was the only man who'd ever made me this insane with wanting.

I cupped the back of his neck with my free hand and opened my mouth under his. Our tongues rolled and stroked, tasting and savoring each other.

Desire flooded my core, causing my cleft to swell and grow damp.

God, this man's kisses were intoxicating, like a drug I couldn't get enough of.

My nipples hardened and my breast pressed against the soft fabric of my lace-trimmed bra. Pre-cum dripped onto my hand as I continued to pump his cock.

Ashur's fingers tugged up the hem of my floor-length dress until he reached the lace edge of my thong. He pushed aside the fabric and teased my aching clit. He circled and rubbed, making my pussy contract.

"You're so wet. God, I can smell your desire. Let me have you, Tara. Let me sate this inferno, and I promise to take my time later."

"Yes." I gasped, arching my neck and allowing Ashur to graze his stubble along my throat.

In the next second my underwear was ripped from my body, and my legs were wrapped around his waist. His six-three frame made it impossible for me to have any control except to hold on.

The blunt tip of his cock slipped past my sopping folds and to the entrance of my pussy. He slowly nudged forward, making me close my eyes at the delicious sting of his erection stretching me.

Fuck, it almost felt like it had when I'd given him my virginity, except this time there was no barrier between us. We were skin to skin. No condom, no contraceptive.

"Oh God," I whimpered. "How the hell did I forget you were hung like a porn star!"

He pulled out and repeated the shallow thrust.

"Damn you're tight." He clenched his jaw, released a heavy breath. "I have to get control or I won't last. I've been waiting for you for two years."

After a few more moments, he pushed a little deeper and then pulled out, rolling the head of his cock around my slick entrance. My body responded instantaneously, growing damper and readier.

Ashur repeated the slow, shallow thrusts and rolls until I thought I would lose my mind.

"Stop teasing me, Ashu," I cried out.

A smile touched his lips, and I realized what I'd called him.

I pulled his head toward me for another deep kiss and then murmured, "I need you to fuck me. Make me regret making us wait."

"Your wish is my command." He slammed into me so hard I saw stars.

My back pressed against the wall, causing my shoulders to rub against the textured wallpaper.

I gasped and moaned with each slide of his cock through my pussy walls. I threw my head back, clutching his shoulders and digging my nails deep.

Ashur hissed and then lightly bit my neck. "If you draw blood, how am I going to explain it?"

"What do you expect? The only thing keeping me on this wall is your cock and a hand on my hip."

"Well let's change that."

Ashur gripped both my ass cheeks, keeping his cock buried deep inside me, and carried me to the bed. He laid me down but remained standing, only leveraging his arms on either side of my head.

"Now I plan to fuck you as I wanted to in my office."

Before I could respond, he pulled out to the tip and slammed back in, setting a hard and fast pace that triggered tiny spasms inside my core.

"Ashu," I whimpered, clutching his body to mine with my thighs. "I'm almost there."

"I know, baby. Come for me." His fingers slid between our bodies to the sensitive nerves of my clitoris.

With the first stroke if his hand, my body detonated. I cried out, convulsing around his pistoning cock. I felt tingles and waves of ecstasy in every cell in my body. I'd waited years to feel this euphoria. This need. I clenched my eyes closed and dug my fingers into his arms, letting the cascade of sensation engulf me.

Ashur pummeled my soaked and spasming core, until his rhythm faltered, causing him to push more of his weight on to my body.

"I can't hold off any longer," he said through gritted teeth as his cock swelled and he followed with his own release, shooting hot spurts of semen into me.

I continued to grip his arms, loving the way his body

flexed above me while the last of his orgasm shot through him.

Watching him come was one of the sexiest things I'd ever encountered.

"I knew it would be like this," Ashur said, gasping for air and staring into my eyes.

"I completely agree."

I slid one hand up to the side of his face and leaned up to kiss him but stopped as a knock sounded on the door, and then it opened.

Ashur and I froze as Samina stormed in. "Ashur, you better get in there or Papa won't make it through the night. And where the fuck is Tar... Oh God, my eyes. Someone kill me now."

"I'm going to leave now and go scrub my eyes with a brillo pad."

We remained still as Samina backed out of the room and closed the door behind her.

"Well that was awkward," I said, not sure whether to be mortified my sister-in-law caught me fucking her brother, or laugh.

"She deserves it after the number of times I've walked in on her and Devin fucking in some random corner of a building. At least we were in our bedroom."

Our bedroom.

Dear God, we'd made love in our bedroom. This was no longer the off-limits place I'd done my best to avoid. I belonged in here as much as he did.

Ashur dropped his head against my shoulder as he steadied his breathing. His cock was still hard and pulsing inside me.

My core contracted, and Ashur lifted his head and grinned.

"Want more, do you?"

"Maybe."

A smile touched my lips as he leaned down and glided his mouth alone mine in soft and gentle passes. I lost myself in him, enjoying his tender kiss. I wanted more, like what we had when we were kids.

All of a sudden, a tinge of panic hit me. This was too intimate, too believable.

What the fuck was I getting myself into?

I broke our kiss and whispered, "We have to stop. Our families are waiting."

Ashur studied me for a second, running a thumb down my throat, making my pulse jump.

"I suppose you're right," he said as he reluctantly pulled from my body and stepped back.

Almost immediately I missed the feel of him, the weight of him, inside me and on me.

He reached over to the side table, grabbed a few facial

tissues, and then handed them to me. Not saying a word, I took them from him and slid off the bed. The slick wetness that coated my thighs brought forth a sense of sadness and want.

I would have his child. I may not conceive today, but soon, and then what?

I wiped his cum from my skin and then tugged my skirt back into place as I walked toward his bathroom.

I couldn't help but gawk as I stepped into the ornate bathroom. This room was extravagant and something out of a magazine.

"I know it's over the top, but you'll get used to it," Ashur said as he followed me inside.

His cock was still hard and jutted out past his bellybutton. His muscular thighs flexed with each step toward me.

A spasm of desire coursed through my body. I was horny and desperate for release again.

I took all of one time to turn me into a nymphomaniac, thinking about the next time I could get his cock inside me.

I blew out an unsteady breath. This was going to be a long evening.

Our gazes locked in the mirror over the sink. Lust and need filled his eyes, and his erection had grown harder.

"Looks like I'll need at least another time to take the edge off."

Moving to the sink, I turned on the water and washed my hands. "We can't."

I dried my hands on the towel hanging from the wall hook and tried to check my makeup. Something that was impossible to do with a very aroused man behind me, who I wanted to fuck me again.

"Tell me you don't want me as much as I want you right now." He braced an arm on either side of the counter around me. "Tell me while we're entertaining the wedding party, you aren't going to think about the slide of my cock inside you or the orgasms you know I can give you."

I licked my kiss-swollen lips. "Ashur, stop."

He crowded me against the granite. He gripped my hips and pulled me against him, letting his thick hot cock burn me through the back of my dress. Leaning down, he grazed his stubble against the side of my neck, and without thought, I closed my eyes and tilted my head.

His hand crept up my abdomen, sending butterflies into my stomach, and then stopped under the swell of my breasts. A finger traced my puckered nipple through my dress, and a moan escaped my lips.

"Do you really want me to stop, Tara?" He pinched the sensitive bud. "Or do you want me to pull your dress up and fuck you for a second time?"

"I... I can't think."

"That's the point."

The air conditioner kicked on, filling the room with cool air and breaking the spell he had me under.

"I have to change." I shifted, slipping from his hold, and walked into the closet.

I stared at racks of clothes, but my mind felt so unfocused that I couldn't figure out what I had to do. This man had me all turned upside down.

Bracing my hand against a wall, I closed my eyes. After a few moments, my brain cells began to fire and I was no longer in a desire-drowned daze. As I turned, I found Ashur watching me with a look that had me taking a step back.

He didn't move, just leaned against the door frame in his naked glory.

"It's only going to get worse."

"What is?"

"The need. I know it will for me."

"You'll just have to resist."

"Why would I do that? Know this, Tara. Now that I've had you, I'm going to want you every chance I get. If you aren't pregnant by the end of the year, it will be a miracle. And even then, when you're swollen with our child, I'll want to fuck you. I've waited years to have you. You're mine and I'm never letting you go."

Ten minutes later, Ashur and I walked out of the master suite. He held my hand in his, running his thumb back and forth over mine.

We'd dressed in silence after he'd made his statement. I wasn't expecting how intense it felt to be with him again. Now I craved more. More than I should ever want. And instead of being annoyed by his possessiveness, I longed to belong to him.

I knew it could never truly happen with all my secrets between us, not to mention the contract.

I should have known better than to enter into a business agreement with a man I'd loved. Now it was too late.

All of a sudden, Ashur stopped, cupped my face, and said, "Breathe, baby."

I stared at him in confusion.

"You're trying to make sense of what you're feeling. Believe me, I get it."

"I..."

He kissed me, silencing my words. "We have a lifetime to figure this out. Let's focus on our friends and family. They're waiting for us."

I nodded my agreement. We weren't going to solve this emotional roller coaster anytime soon.

"Plus, I have a bet with Veer to see who will be the first person to leave the room when they can't handle Papa's antics."

I couldn't help but smile. "My money is on Samina or me."

He tilted my face up so I could gaze in his amber depths. "No, love, you have more tolerance than you should with the man. You got that trait from your mom. All my money is on Samina. I think Papa's presence incites violence in her."

I had to give him that one. Sam was so controlled in every situation except when it came to her father. And Minesh Kumar had a knack for pushing her buttons. "I'll say she'll crack within the first ten minutes."

"I counter that it'll be less than five."

"Is that a bet?" I laughed.

He ran a finger up from the base of my throat to my lips as a wicked glint entered his eyes. "Absolutely."

"The stakes?"

"Winner's choice. As long as it's something sexual."

Immediately arousal shot through me. Shit, this man could say one thing and I got wet.

"Deal." I offered him my hand.

CHAPTER TEN

"Breathe, Tara," I whispered to myself as my heavily embroidered bridal *dupatta* was set on my head.

One hour and counting. One hour until I'd take on my role as first lady. One hour until I'd officially become Ashur's wife and have the funds to buy Ameera back.

My stomach clenched. Exactly at noon today, my net worth would become a hundred times greater.

I wasn't a pauper but any means. The money I'd amassed over the years through my law practice and my work for Solon would make it so I could live a fabulous life without working another single day for the rest of my life. But all my money wasn't enough to qualify to bid for Ameera in the auction. And even though Solon had more money than anyone could imagine, there was no way the organization could enter the auction without revealing itself. The only way they could help was by manipulating technology and providing manpower when an operation was activated. Solon's board constantly monitored any leads or rumors on her whereabouts. The second they received credible news Ameera, they'd deploy my team. The auction and the endless coordination was actually our contingency plan.

A wave of guilt hit me. What was Ameera doing at this moment, while I was covered in a million dollars of jewelry, getting ready to marry a man for his billions?

God, I'd fallen so far from the girl with dreams of white picket fences. Instead of marrying for love as I'd always imagined, I was using Ashur for money. Yes, he was the one who offered, and the sex was an added bonus, but when it came down to it, I wouldn't have agreed to marry him if it wasn't for his money.

I'd become the whore who only wanted Ashur for his bank account as Minesh Kumar had accused me of when I was eighteen.

"Ms. Zain, you're all set. Your bridesmaids will be here momentarily," my wedding stylist said as she clasped the last pin into my *dupatta*. "Want another bottle of water?"

"No, I'm good. Thanks for making my vision come to life."

"It was my pleasure." Dara gave me a beaming smile. "I'm honored Ms. Neya chose me to be your wedding attendant."

"Maybe I can convince her to lend you to me for all my events."

"I would love that." She checked her watch. "My ride will arrive in a few minutes. Is there anything I can do for you before I leave?"

"No." I shook my head. "I think a few moments to calm the nerves is all I need."

"I never expected you to suffer from a case of anxiety. You're always so poised."

I almost snorted but kept it inside. It wouldn't have been ladylike to make bodily sounds.

"Don't tell me you bought into the ice-for-a-heart crap the media like to say."

"No. I've worked for Neya for years and she would never design anything for someone she couldn't stand." She smiled. "Plus, I've seen the way you and Mr. Kumar look at each other when you think no one is watching. There is nothing cold about the fire burning between you two."

My cheeks heated and my body tingled remembering how hard Ashur had fucked me yesterday.

Before I could respond, she spoke again. "You soften him. When he was running, many of us wondered if we could vote for a man who kept such a tight rein on his emotions. To go from a president who was ruled by temper and volatility to one that was so cold that it didn't bother him when people referred to him as an asshole was a hard pill to swallow."

"He was never an asshole. There are just things in his past that make him cautious."

Like what happened when we were kids, and then of course everything he'd experienced during his three tours in the Air Force.

A throat cleared, and we both turned in Casey's direction.

"Your bridesmaids are on their way up, and Ms. Dara's car has arrived."

We said a quick goodbye as Dara gather her belongings and then exited with Casey behind her.

Taking a deep breath, I turned my attention back to my reflection in the mirror in front of the dressing table.

My long black hair was curled in large ringlets and fastened under my *dupatta*. My face had a natural glow that wasn't natural at all. My makeup artist, Walter, had told me the idea was to look like I woke up gorgeous, even when my real face was hiding somewhere underneath five layers of makeup. The one thing I had wanted over the top was my eyes. I loved the artistry of doing intricate eye makeup, so I'd asked Walter to match the colors of my gown. And he hadn't disappointed.

Yes, it wasn't demure as was expected of the first lady, but I couldn't care less. My wedding day, my way.

With the combination of Neya's amazing wedding

outfit, Dara's hair expertise, and Walter's makeup magic, I looked like I was walking off the pages of a Bollywood wedding magazine.

The only thing missing was a debonair groom. And I'd be meeting him in... I glanced at the clock. In forty-nine minutes.

After Ashur had fucked my brains out almost a day ago, we hadn't seen or spoken to each other. He'd been called into an important meeting within minutes of entering the wedding party meeting. Whatever had happened had consumed all of his time for the rest of the day.

His absence had left me to man the family, friends, and guests. Minesh's disposition hadn't improved in the slightest, and so for the most part, everyone pretended to ignore his antics.

And true to Ashur's prediction, Samina lasted all of three minutes before she walked out of the meeting room for a shot of tequila. I guess I owed Ashur a debt now.

The thing that sucked the most was to attend our rehearsal dinner with a big chunk of my wedding party missing. That's what had happened when all my closest friends had decided to enter the political world.

Whatever had gone down must have been major. I'd almost given in to the urge to call in a few of my contacts in Solon to get the details, but restrained myself. Any snooping outside of Ameera's case would undermine

Tyler. The second I got nosy was the second I'd convey I didn't have confidence in Tyler's ability to handle his role as director. Solon had never had a director who held a high-level government position until Tyler, and because of this, he had to walk a very tight rope between the two roles.

My phone rang, and I grabbed it from the counter. My stomach flipped when I saw who the caller was.

"Hello, Mr. President."

"Hello, First Lady."

The possessive way he said those words had a shiver going down my spine.

Why did it feel so good to hear his voice?

Maybe because you haven't gone more than half a day without talking to him in the last eighteen months.

"I'm sorry I left you to the family yesterday."

"I'll think of some way for you to make it up to me."

"I'm sure you will."

"Ash, is everything okay?"

He blew out a deep breath. "Not really but there's nothing I can do."

I wanted to ask him to elaborate but knew he couldn't tell me. Was this what other political wives felt?

I was as nosy as they came and not knowing the nitty gritty of a situation only piqued my curiosity more.

How does one go from being the boss to the woman behind the man? I understood that I couldn't handle missions anymore, but I couldn't even practice law. I was a kickass lawyer, but no one would see that now that I'd be Ashur's wife.

Snap out of it, Tara. Stop thinking about your change in circumstances and focus on being there for the man who seems more stressed than he should be on his wedding day.

"We can stay in Washington so you can handle whatever crisis is going on. I won't be upset if we have to cancel our honeymoon."

"God, no. It's the only thing keeping this day on the right track. I want a few days alone with you where I'm not the president. I just want to be a man spending time with his wife. Will you let me be your husband? Will you for a few days pretend there are no bargains or financial gains? That there is no contract stipulating a baby? That you and I are a couple who are completely into each other?"

I swallowed. Dear God. What could have happened? Ashur never sounded so vulnerable. It was as if he was resigned to a complete and inevitable fallout.

"Whatever's going on, I'm not going anywhere. You're stuck with me, Mr. President."

He released another sigh, then said, "Fuck. I just messed up my hair. That battle ax in charge of my attire is going to kick my ass."

"Ashu, I can't believe you're afraid of Neya. She barely comes to your shoulder."

When Neya had said she would make sure Ashur was dressed the way a president should dress for his wedding,

I'd almost felt sorry for Ashur. Neya was the epitome of tiny but mighty. No one got in the way of her fashion sense, even a six-foot-three president.

"I'm afraid of you, and you're shorter than her."

"Whatever," I muttered.

"Besides, I know things about her the average Joe would never know."

"Like what?"

All the fine hairs on my arm prickled. He couldn't know she worked for Solon.

"The same thing you're hiding."

"And that is?" I probed.

"That both of you are fifth-degree black belts in jujitsu."

Relief washed over me.

"Who told you?"

"I have my sources."

There was only one person who would threaten the president without fear of consequences. And she was the one who promised retribution for the exhausting night we'd had last night.

"Sam told you. That girl was planning painful ways to make you pay last night."

Ashur laughed. "Yes. She actually threatened that Neya would literally kick my ass with her mad skills if I left her alone with Papa ever again."

"Samina and I were thinking along the same lines. But

it wasn't Neya who I envisioned kicking your ass, it was me."

"Is that a challenge?"

"Absolutely. Name the time and place."

He chuckled and I knew the little fun banter had eased whatever tension that was weighing on his shoulders.

"The last thing I plan to do on my honeymoon is fight with my wife. My goal is to fuck her senseless."

His words brought forth all the dirty, naked fantasies I'd harbored for Ashur over the past fifteen years.

"Umm...okay." I licked my lips.

Images of him pounding into me flashed in my mind.

Dammit, Tara. You're supposed to counsel him, not think about fucking him.

I had to get myself on sane ground if I was going to make it through the wedding reception.

"I have an idea."

"The answer is no."

"But you haven't even heard my suggestion."

"Ashur, I know what you're thinking, and no, we can't skip our own wedding."

"How did you figure those were my thoughts?"

"Because I remember what you were like after we slept together when we were younger. You wanted to skip every gathering, party, or event to get laid. I know you."

"You're probably the only person who does."

His tone had changed back to the worried one.

I guessed it didn't matter that it was the president's wedding day—he still had a twenty-four/seven job to do.

"Ash, are you sure you're okay?"

"There are things I can't discuss with you, but it means a lot that you care enough to ask."

There was a touch of longing to his response that made my heart contract.

"I understand." Probably more than he realized.

I had so many secrets that I wasn't sure how Ashur would react once he found all of them out. I wanted to believe he'd stand by me and fight for me if he ever learned what I was or had done, but there was always something in the back of my mind making me think I couldn't depend on him.

"Tara?"

"Yes."

"Do you think we can ever get back to what we lost when we were young?"

Why was he saying this when he was the one who wanted an iron-clad agreement stating where he stood on our relationship?

"Ashur, I don't know what you want me to say. I have no idea what will happen between us. There's a lot of history. I'm not that girl anymore and neither are you the boy I knew."

"I just wish sometimes that I'd questioned all the shit

Papa had said about you. I wish I'd fought for us a little more."

"I wished that for a long time too. But we can't change the past, Ash. All we can do is not fall into the same traps again."

"I suppose."

What the hell was going on that he sounded so vulnerable? Where was the man that took no shit from anyone? The one who scared the crap out of friend and foe alike?

I wanted to reach through the phone and tell him it would be okay, even though I knew I couldn't do it.

"We can have a happy life together. Everything else we'll figure out as we go."

He remained quiet for a moment, then spoke. "I want to tear the contract up. I want it to be the way we were before all the shit Papa put us through. I want you to love me the way you did when you were eighteen. I want it about to be about us, not the election or the money I promised you."

Oh God. I couldn't do this right now.

Dammit Ashur, why now? Why not two years ago?

"Ash, we can't go back in time. Our reality is that we have an agreement."

"I know. I'm telling you what I thought. I'd understand your hesitation after what I'd said when we signed the contract. I shouldn't have told you it was only ever going to be business with a side of sex. I was an asshole. I must be more like him than I believed."

"You're not an asshole. And you're nothing like him."

"I am."

I could hear Neya saying something, and I knew Ash was in trouble.

"Okay, I have to go. Neya is glaring at me and has a spray bottle and a comb to make me look presentable."

"Good luck." I laughed and the tension of the second earlier disappeared. "Ashur?"

"Yes."

"I'll see you in a few. I'll be the girl wearing enough jewelry to blind everyone in sight and expensive enough to fund a small country for ten years."

"I'm sure you'll look beautiful, Commander."

We hung up and I closed my eyes.

I was doing the right thing by not getting his hopes up, by not telling him I wanted to make it real. Then why did I feel like shit?

Because it's not him you're protecting, it's you.

At that moment, Jacinta walked in with a tray of shots and set them on a table near me. "Dear God. You're beautiful."

"Thank you." I gave her a weary smile.

"What's wrong?"

"Nerves." It wasn't a complete lie but a believable one.

"Here, take one, but don't fuck up your lipstick or Walter will kick our asses."

I took the shot of tequila she handed me and then downed it in one gulp.

"Give me another."

Just as I reached for more liquid courage, Samina entered my dressing room. She had Mira cocked on her side, while the little angel cooed and played with the necklace on her mother's neck.

"Woman, you're pregnant," Samina said, shifting Mira from one hip to the other. "Do you know the shit the press will say if they get a picture of a very pregnant Senator Camden-George with alcohol?"

"Probably something like my conservative morals have been swayed by marrying a liberal." Jacinta gave Sam a nonchalant wave and took a seat in an empty chair next to me.

She tugged at the material along her very large belly and then rubbed her stomach. She was gorgeous on a normal day with her long, always well-groomed blond hair, Amazon height, and supermodel features, but pregnant she glowed.

"You make it look so easy." I leaned over grabbed a bottle of water and sucked through the straw Walter had put in it so I wouldn't ruin my lipstick. Hopefully he wouldn't make a surprise inspection and find the shot glass on the counter. "In fact, both of you do. I don't think either of you has complained about nausea or morning sickness."

"Just you wait. I've never seen you do anything without rocking any endeavor. Pregnancy won't be any different." Jacinta reached out, plucked the bottle from my fingers, and then took a sip.

"From your lips to God's ears."

I had a feeling when my time came I wouldn't be so lucky.

"Why are we talking about babies? You have to get married first." Samina pulled her necklace out of Mira's mouth and handed her a teething ring. "She might be knocked up now. Especially since she's been secretly going at it with my brother the whole time."

Well, hell. Let's tell the world I was boning Ashur.

Bitch.

"Cat got your tongue?" Sam smirked.

Before I could respond, Casey walked in, signaling that it was time for the wedding.

CHAPTER ELEVEN

The next few hours were a blur.

I remembered walking down the aisle, the feel of goosebumps prickling my skin when Ashur took my hand and whispered, "You're mine," and the chaste but potent kiss at the end of the ceremony. After that, I felt like I was living in someone else's body. I couldn't remember how many people I met or the number of photos I'd taken.

I should have expected the chaos of hours upon hours of conversation, hugs, and well wishes. I dealt with people all day, many of them celebrities, but living the life of one was overwhelming. Thankfully, I'd changed out of my thirty-pound lengha and put on a lighter-weight, more modern dress that resembled a high-fashion American wedding gown with Indian embroidered accents. It had allowed me to move freely and gave me a slight bit of comfort.

Ashur, on the other hand, seemed calm and watchful. He'd smiled and interacted but his mind was occupied. I could tell he wanted to slip away to take care of business multiple times over the night. He'd kept me by his side, contently touching me or holding my hand. It was as if he needed me to ground him. Around the time the majority of the guests had left, he'd slipped away for some last-minute meetings. But not before he'd laid a mind-blowing kiss on me that had a caused a stir and a round of applause.

Now I was sitting inside Air Force One waiting for Ashur and surrounded by security. This was not how I ever expected to go on my honeymoon. It would have been lower key, with less press, and anonymity.

Then again, that dream of marriage had died the day I'd left Houston for Boston.

God, how had I ended up here, married to the man who'd made me swear off marriage and happily ever after?

I laughed to myself, gaining curious looks from some of the agents. Ignoring them, I stared out the window at the empty tarmac. Well, with the exception of all the military and security personnel monitoring the plane.

"Mrs. Kumar," Jake, the agent Casey had assigned as my personal security, said from my side.

The fine hairs on the back of my neck prickled. Holy Shit, I was no longer Tara Zain. I was Tara Zain Kumar. The First Lady of the United States.

"President Kumar said he apologizes for the delay and will be a few more minutes."

"Thank you."

Twenty minutes later, when Ashur finally arrived on the plane, there was worry and uncertainty etched all over his face. I wanted to go to him, find some way to comfort him or at least ask him if I could do anything. But stopped when Veer and Tyler came on board. Veer handed Ashur a stack of papers and began to talk.

Tyler came toward me with a bleak look in his eyes told me something was wrong.

Oh God. Something had happened with Ameera.

"Have a good time on your vacation, T-Rex," Tyler said in his pretentious happy Louisiana gentile twang. The one I'd told him sounded like a Southern used car salesman. Then he walked over to me and gave me a hug.

"Everything is in place. Once you get home, we'll prep for the auction."

"What about the leads on Ameera?"

"We think she is in Pakistan in the same area where the girls were held two years ago."

"I supposed it was too much to hope that we'd have an exact location. There's no telling where in the mountains they are holding Ame."

"The second they pinpoint her, I will notify you." A dangerous gleam entered his eyes.

"Don't do anything until I get back. You can't take the risk."

"Yes, Commander."

I glared at him. "I mean it, Tyler. I know you'll want to go in guns blazing, but right now too many people are watching you."

"You're still the boss, Tara. At least for this operation anyway. You're lead and I'll take orders from you. Besides, I'm hoping you change your mind and keep me from taking over a job that could be viewed as treason."

I rolled my eyes. "Unless you sell government secrets to another nation, I think you're safe."

"I'm serious. You don't have to quit. There is a clause that gives you the option to change your mind."

"Who told you?"

"No one. I signed the same contract. The board refuses to let any of their agents go without a fight."

"It's not their decision."

"No, it's yours. Make sure you're making the right choice for you, not for who you think you should be."

"Ty," I whispered. "All I've ever known is Solon. But I know as well as you do that I can't have a life with Ashur if I'm helping break the laws he's sworn to uphold. I have to protect him and his presidency. And the best way to do this is by not being any more of a liability than I already am."

"All I ask is that you don't make any rash decisions you'll wish you hadn't later."

The problem was that I'd regret not giving Ashur and I a chance if I stayed in Solon.

"When have I ever made a decision without thinking it through?"

At my words, Tyler gave me his "are you serious?" look and gestured to the area around us. "Would you be here if you thought through your relationship with Ashur?"

"It was a lot more rational than you believe."

"Keep lying to yourself. I know why you agreed to marry him. Do you?"

I swallowed, glancing at Ashur, who was still engrossed in his conversation with Veer.

"Drop it," I ordered.

"Fine. We have enough shit to worry about besides your refusal to admit you're still in love with Ashur."

I clenched my jaw.

"I really want to punch you right now."

A grin crossed Tyler's face. "Too bad you have to be prim and proper now that you're the first lady."

"Whatever," I muttered. "I'm heading to a cabin in the woods. There is nothing prim and proper about it."

"It's still a vacation. Your first in years, if I remember correctly."

"Pot, meet kettle," I stated. "If you recall, my last

vacation was with you and Ameera on that beach in the Maldives after the South African assignment."

"I remember." Tyler's voice grew serious.

"Ty, why haven't you ever told her how you feel?"

"Because she wasn't ready to hear it."

"So, you let her think this thing between you two was just sex?"

"It was never just sex." He clenched his jaw. "She just refused to see it for anything else."

I shook my head. "Once she's home, it's time you two had a long talk."

"Oh, believe me. We are going to talk."

I heard Ashur clear his throat and glanced over Tyler's shoulder, catching Ashur watching us. Under the exhaustion in his eyes was a desire that had my body responding.

"Time to go, boys," Ashur said as he continued to stare at me. "I'd like to leave before we have another crisis that needs my attention."

Veer came up to me. "Have fun, T-Rex. Keep him in line. And don't let him boss you around."

I shot Tyler a glare. "You got him saying it too?"

Tyler shrugged and said, "It fits. Would you rather I have everyone say Commander?"

The fact I'd gotten the name during a mission when I'd punched a guy three times my size was something he'd never share, so it made me wonder what story he'd weaved for the nickname. That would be something else I'd have to ask him about after I returned.

I growled at him, "One day I'm going to make you pay."

"Give it your best shot, shorty."

I almost told him that I'd knocked him on his ass before and would do it again, but stopped myself.

"You two are like siblings. Sometimes I think you're more his sister than Jaci." Veer draped his arm around my shoulder. "Too bad for him, you belong to Sam and me. We knew you first, so we get to claim you."

"Wrong. I knew her before you." Ashur came up to my other side. "That means she belongs to me."

His words triggered the memory of how we'd met. I'd come into Kumar Industries to have lunch with my father. I'd run into Ashur as I rushed out of the elevators on Dad's floor. He'd helped me up and then carried the bags of food I'd brought to the floor's break room.

He'd charmed me and had asked me out within five minutes. As an eighteen-year-old, I was totally enchanted by the older twenty-three-year-old. It wasn't until my father had caught us walking down the hall that I realized I'd agreed to a date with the heir apparent of Kumar industries. It hadn't mattered to me so we began to see each other. Our relationship had gone from casual dating to falling love and planning a future within months.

If it hadn't been for Minesh Kumar's interference, we'd

have more than likely still been together. Sometimes I missed the naive girl who hadn't realized love doesn't conquer all. The old Tara had been so carefree and full of dreams. The kind I couldn't imagine today. The ones with a thriving law practice, a husband who was head over heels in love with her, a home in suburbia, and at least four children.

"Care to get your hands off my wife?"

Veer dropped his arm and held his hand up. "Married less than a few hours and you've become a Neanderthal. Welcome to the club."

"That's what we men do when we find our women. It's ingrained in our DNA," Tyler added and then fist bumped both Ashur and Veer.

"I've got the Three Stooges here..." I rolled my eyes. "Why are you part of this exchange? You're not even married yet."

"*Yet* is the operative word," Tyler countered.

"So, no luck convincing the pretty UN ambassador you want more than just in her pants?" Veer asked with a grin.

A dark look passed through Tyler's eyes. "The second she's back from her assignment, I'm going to lock her in a room and make it very clear where we stand."

Okay, we couldn't go there. Not with Ameera being God knew where.

"How the three of you convinced the voters you were progressive on women's issues is beyond me."

"There's a difference between believing in equal pay, reproductive rights, and opportunities and wanting to keep another man's fingers off my wife."

I glowered at Ashur, who only grinned and set a hand on the small of my back, pulling me to his side and kissing the top of my head.

My heart skipped a beat. This man was breathtaking when he smiled. The shadows seemed to be lifting, and the tension Ashur walked onto the plane with appeared to have eased.

That was when I realized how genuinely deep the friendship between Tyler, Veer, and Ashur really was and that the silly banter had been deliberate.

If it wouldn't have pissed off my caveman husband, I'd throw my arms around Veer and Tyler and give them both big kisses.

Aaron the flight attendant spoke from behind us. "Sir, the captain said we are ready to leave as soon as you are."

"That's your cue to get lost." Ashur gestured toward the door and the service stairs. "Don't start a war before I come back."

"That's your job, so don't worry." Veer smirked and left with Tyler right behind him.

CHAPTER TWELVE

I shook awake, searching for something to grab onto. Gripping the textured fabric of the sofa armrest, I focused on the area around me.

I was alone in this part of the cabin. The staff was nowhere in sight and all I could hear was the rumble of voices behind the partition separating my section of the plane from the front half.

How long had I slept?

I checked my watch and realized it was close to midnight. We'd been flying for two and a half hours.

I guessed the exhaustion of the last few days had finally caught up to me.

The last thing I'd remembered was Ashur sitting next to me for takeoff. He hadn't released my hand from the moment Veer and Tyler deplaned. It was as if he feared I'd leave.

I wasn't the one he should worry about leaving. He was the one who would have to decide if he could live with what I'd spent most of my adult life doing. I only hoped he would understand that my work, even if some of it was illegal, had saved the lives of countless men, women, and children.

My gut told me he'd find out my involvement in Solon sooner rather than later.

God, please Ameera's rescue go as planned.

So far everything was set for a week after we returned from Texas, but things could change in the blink of an eye.

It took all my will to resist the urge to pull out the secured phone I'd hidden in my clutch, log into the Solon network, and double check everything was going according to the logistics I'd laid out.

For now, the team was in a holding pattern, keeping an eye out for any changes but waiting for the auction. In a few hours the funds would transfer to the Swiss account I'd given Ameera's captors, and Tyler would receive the access codes to enter next week's auction.

My heart sank thinking of how Ashur's money would give me the ability to free Ameera. He'd offered me his fortune when I'd agreed to marry him, but I'd never thought I'd actually have to use it. Now, I was no better than any other woman who married a man for his riches.

I uncurled myself and sat up, pushing the blanket covering me down to my lap.

Releasing a deep sigh, I stood and went toward the lavatory to freshen up. I quietly stepped around the partition, trying not to disturb the heavy discussion Ashur was engaged in with some of the Secret Service agents.

His short hair was a bit messy, telling me he'd run his fingers through it over and over again. His telltale sign that he was thinking through a difficult topic.

He was still sexy as hell even with the hard set of his jaw and lips.

I could almost feel his mouth on me. The kiss he'd given me at our reception had me craving more of his intoxicating taste.

Would I always feel this way?

Who was I kidding—it hadn't waned in fifteen years. I doubted the attraction would ever stop.

A bit of turbulence shook the plane, making me realize I was dawdling. I took the hallway and walked into the bathroom.

The walls were a toasted beige with a scent of fresh paint and every fixture, from the faucets to the lights, was a styled oil-rubbed bronze. The space was big, almost five times the size of the lavatories on commercial jetliners.

The bathroom was designed to feel and look like a proper bathroom, including a shower. A luxury for the first family to enjoy when traveling.

Setting my toiletry bag on the counter, I washed my face, dried it, and then reapplied my makeup.

Just as I was finishing up, Ashur walked in and leaned against the door frame.

"Want to christen Air Force One?"

I scrunched my face in an "ew." "Nope. Besides, I'm pretty sure all kinds of lewd things have been done on here in the past. I don't want to add to it."

He walked toward me and set an arm on either side of me, while staring at my lips. "Are you sure? The way I see it, my wife needs something and I want to give it to her."

"Your wife is fine, thank you."

"I felt your hunger, Tara. This is only a hint of what I've gone through the past two years."

I held his gaze, hoping he hadn't noticed my dilated pupils. "You're mistaken."

Those beautiful lips of his quirked at the sides. "Let me check."

He dropped to his haunches and gripped my stocking-covered ankle.

"I love these fuck-me heels you wear. Makes me think of all kinds of dirty things."

"They're practical, nothing fuck-me about them."

"I disagree. The way you walk in them incites visions of bending you over the nearest surface. The way you own the room while wearing them, makes any man that sees you want nothing more than to rumple the incredibly controlled and sexy Ms. Zain."

"Mrs. Kumar." My breath felt heavy and my mouth parched.

"That's right. Mrs. Kumar. I've waited a long time to hear that from your lips." He glided his hand along the inside of my leg, over my knees, and to the juncture of my sopping cleft.

"We can't, Ashur."

"What can't we, Tara? All I'm doing is making sure my wife isn't lying about her needs."

He grazed the wet fabric of my underwear, and I clamped my thighs to block him from going further. "Not here."

He licked his lips, "Yes here. Let me taste you. Let me fuck my tongue into your hot, wet pussy."

My knees grew weak. What would it be like to have his mouth on me, in me, all over me?

I needed him to touch me, but not like this. There was no doubt I'd lose myself to the pleasure, forgetting anything but the orgasms he would give me. And then, I wouldn't want it to stop there. I'd beg him to fuck me, and I didn't want our first time as a married couple to be in the bathroom of a plane that belonged to the United States government.

"Please, not here. Maybe in the future, but not tonight." I looked down to where he knelt.

The plea in my voice must have broken through the lust, and he sighed. He tugged his hand free, stood and pulled me against him, my back to his aroused front.

I grasped the arm he had across my body and then leaned my head against his shoulder, inhaling in short pants, unable to stop the unsteadiness of my breath.

"Look at us in the mirror."

I lifted my head and studied Ashur's giant body behind me. He towered over my small frame, but somehow, we fit.

We'd always fit.

He regarded me with hooded eyes that were filled with longing.

"I'm not going to be fucking you in here. I won't take that from us. When I take you, it isn't going to be a fast fuck. It is going to be long, hot, and sweaty."

Relief washed over me. He had me so worked up that I probably would have let him. At least, one of us had some restraint.

"However, we aren't going out there until I see you coming at least once."

Strike the restraint part.

"Ashur, no."

He tugged the fitted hem of my dress up my thighs and over my bottom.

Why wasn't I pushing his hands away? Why was I stepping a little wider?

Because you want the release as much as he wants to give it to you.

"You're so wet, baby. I can see your desire soaking your underwear."

I glance toward the closed door. "I'm not quiet. I don't want anyone to hear us."

His hand crept down to the waistband of my thong, ducking inside.

"Why don't you let me worry about that. You just enjoy."

His fingers grazed my clit, sending a shockwave of desire down my spine.

I gasped, "Ashu."

"Are you watching us?"

"Yes," I whispered.

I couldn't keep my gaze away from us, even if I wanted to. He was so sure, so confident, so fucking sexy as hell.

He repeated the feathery touch, not going farther than the sensitive nub. He teased me until I closed my eyes and surrendered to his soft caress. He pushed a finger past my dipping cleft and into my aching core, making me gasp and writhe against him.

"Watch yourself, Tara. You are a goddess, a warrior, the siren who calls to me in my dreams. See what I see, when you come."

I opened my lids and focused on my face. My cheeks were flushed and my eyes glazed. My chest heaved up and down within the constraints of my bra. My nipples rubbed against the lace fabric covering them, causing them to pebble tight. The front of my underwear that was soaked through with my arousal.

My fingers dug into his arm, holding on for dear life.

Ashur's hand worked me underneath the material, pumping in and out, pressing at the sensitive area deep inside, and driving me crazy.

"Do you want to come, love?"

"Yes, Ashu. I... I... need. I'm dying."

"No, you're not. You're about to shatter on my hand. Now let me see it." He plunged another digit inside me to join the other.

My body bowed, loving the pleasure-pain of his thick fingers stretching me and working my soaping pussy.

I rode his fingers, my head thrashing back and forth. Just when my body couldn't hold out any longer, I turned my face, gripped the back of his head, and captured his lips. My pussy contracted and then clamped down on his pistioning fingers. My orgasm took over, making my body shudder and shake. I clamped my eyes closed and cried out my pleasure into Ashur's mouth as my release flooded his fingers in my cum. He continued his ministrations until he'd wrung the last of my release out of my spasming pussy.

I lost the ability to hold myself up and collapsed completely against Ashur, breaking our kiss. He held me to him, murmuring words I couldn't really understand into my hair.

Slowly he slid out of my still-convulsing core. "Now Mrs. Kumar. I believe we need to prepare ourselves for landing."

I nodded but was unable to move. Even when Ashur reached to the side, grabbed a napkin, and cleaned his hand and my thighs.

"I love how wet you get for me. Like I said, there's no hiding your need from me."

I gave an incoherent hum and kept my eyes closed.

"I believe you're orgasm drunk." He kissed the top of my head.

Was there such a thing? Who cared? I couldn't even muster the strength to stand on my feet.

Ashur kept me in his arms for a few minutes longer, letting my mind come back to reality.

"We need to go back, love."

"Okay. Give me a second."

I inhaled slow, long breaths until I could finally focus.

Then, I turned in his arms, wrapping them around his neck. "Thank you for the orgasm, Mr. President."

He smiled, resting his forehead against mine. "You're welcome, First Lady."

I cupped his erection, squeezing it. "Do you want me to return the favor?"

"I want nothing else at the moment, but we can't. Everyone on the other side of the door—" he gestured with his head, "—knows we were up to something in here. Let's not give them more to discuss."

Well hell, that was going to be awkward.

"You started it. It's your fault."

He stepped back, offering me his hand. "This is the one thing I will happily take the blame for."

CHAPTER THIRTEEN

A little before two thirty in the morning, I leaned against the giant bay window of the den of the cabin Ashur and I would share for the next few days and watched the last of the agents conduct their final check of the building before closing the door behind them.

Even though I hated the constant protection, I understood it was a necessity. The media had swarmed the Austin–Bergstrom International Airport, wanting a glimpse of the president and first lady. Some had even gone as far as jumping the fences and triggering the remotely activated cameras and security monitors in the hanger we were supposed to use. Thankfully no one outside of our Secret Service was aware we had a planted decoy who led them to Jacinta's large estate instead of the large cabin where Ashur and I would spend our honeymoon.

It wasn't considered remote by Texas standards, since it was just an hour and a half outside of Austin, but it was far enough removed to provide the security needed to enjoy our time together without the worry of a camera taking a picture of us. For the next few days, there would be no state visits, no official duties, and no media.

For me anyway. Technically, I was jobless.

Ashur would still have to attend a daily briefing with Veer and Tyler.

The clank of ice in glass had my gaze moving from the closed front door of the cabin and across the den to where Ashur stood at the bar. He was barefoot in only his suit pants and a button-down shirt.

He was sexy down to his toes.

How could a man's toes look appealing?

The muscles of his broad back bunched and moved as he picked up a crystal decanter. He poured a few fingers of his favorite scotch, dropped in an orange peel, and then swirled the aromatic liquid. He took a deep gulp and closed his eyes, savoring the taste of his concoction.

He was fascinating to watch. His movements were so calm, as if he hadn't a care in the world and was ready for a relaxing evening in. When in fact he carried the weight of our country on his shoulders.

Would we ever get to a place where we'd share everything? It scared me that I wouldn't have the type of relationship my parents shared. Could a relationship survive if we both kept secrets?

Slowly, Ashur set his empty glass on the bar counter and turned to face me. His eyes were filled with desire, but there was also a glint of something else I couldn't put my finger on but made a throbbing pulse deep inside my core.

My heart pounded into my ears and my breath grew shallow.

This was it.

Goosebumps prickled my skin.

Why was I so nervous? We'd technically consummated our marriage the other night, and the interlude aboard Air Force One wasn't any less intimate.

Maybe it was because the world had watched me marry Ashur in the gardens of the White House. Effectively turning us into an American royal romance. Or the fact there was no turning back now. I was his wife for better or worse.

There was no turning back the moment I'd agreed to marry him.

Now, here we were, about to have our wedding night.

"Tara," Ashur said as he came up to me, setting his hands on my waist.

My nipples immediately responded to my name and pebbled into hard buds.

He lifted my hair and set it on one shoulder as he grazed his evening stubble on the side of my neck.

"We can be good together. Give us a chance. I meant what I said on the phone today. I want to make this real."

I swallowed, holding in the desire I felt as tears prickled the backs of my eyes.

"What about our history?"

"Leave it there. I don't want anything in the way of our future."

There was no way he'd feel the same once he learned that I'd lived a double life for the past ten years. That I was still living a double life.

"I wish it were that easy. It takes time."

"I know." He sighed. "Then will you pretend for our time here that we are ordinary people who are in love, who want to spend time together just learning each other. I need this, Tara. I need you. The moment we get back, all hell—"

I turned in his arms, cupped his face, and covered his lips with mine, silencing anything else he had to say. I couldn't hear it. The longing in his words was destroying me.

This hard man felt so much. The least I could do was give him what he asked, if only for a few days.

I only hoped my heart would survive.

Ashur gripped my bottom, lifting me against him and deepening the kiss. The hard, thick ridge of his cock pressed into the juncture of my cleft, and my core drowned with desire. His tongue invaded my mouth, rubbing against mine in a seductive rhythm that made my clit swell and ache.

I dug my fingers into his hair and pressed even closer. I wanted him to consume me in whatever way he desired. I wanted him to make me forget about anything other than him and what we shared in this cabin.

My back hit a wall, allowing me to wrap my legs around his waist.

"Ash," I murmured, trying to work my hand between us so I could undo his shirt buttons. I was desperate to feel him skin to skin.

"No, not here." He pulled back, grabbing my hand and placing it on his chest before gazing at me through a desire-filled haze.

"Why not?" I whined, wanting nothing more than the delicious feel of his cock bare against my pussy.

With breath coming in hard pants and eyes dilated, he said with a gruff voice, "The windows aren't covered and I'll be damned if I let anyone see you naked but me."

Immediately, I glanced to the side and glimpsed our security monitoring the perimeter of the area.

"Well, that's inconvenient."

"Immensely."

I unclasped my ankles from around him and dropped them to the floor, stepping out of his hold. Confusion crossed his face and I couldn't help but smile.

Did he think I wanted to stop? Hell no.

I offered him my hand. "Let's go, soldier. I want to get naked in private."

He slid his palm over mine and tugged me toward him, sealing our lips for another circuit-breaking kiss. Once he had his fill, he whispered, "I'm an airman, not a soldier. Air Force, not Army."

"My mistake." I hummed, sucking his lower lip into my mouth and then popping it free.

"You said that on purpose."

I grinned and turned, guiding him toward the master suite.

With each step, my arousal grew and the pulse between my legs felt like unending torment. I was almost positive that if he barely grazed my clit, I'd go off. The orgasm on the plane had done nothing for the low pulse of desire that seemed to burn inside me whenever he was near.

God, I was addicted. The need for him flowed in my veins and the only way to settle my ache for him was to fuck him senseless.

"Tara?"

I glanced over my shoulder, noticing him adjust his thick erection. "When we enter that room, you're no longer boss."

My steps faltered.

He caught me before I fell, pressing my ass into the hard ridge of his cock.

I gripped his hips, leaning into his heat. "When have I been the boss?"

He laughed against my ear. "Tara, I've let you control every aspect of our relationship since we made our agreement. I've gone two years without sex because of your no-sex rule."

How could that be?

"But we've only been together a year and a half."

"Let's say I knew I was going to marry you and didn't want anyone else's cunt on my cock but yours."

His crudeness should have pissed me off, but for some crazy reason, it made the need burning inside me intensify.

"Ash."

"Ashu," He countered, walking us toward our bedroom door.

"Why is it so important I call you that?"

"Because when you say it, I know what it really means."

How could he know what it meant, when I had no clue?

I turned in his arms as we passed through the doorway.

Not caring to study the room, I focused on the sexy-as-sin man before me and the statement he'd made.

"What does it mean?"

"You'll figure it out soon enough." The lock clicked and a wicked glint entered his eyes.

"We don't need to lock the door. The only people in this cabin are the two of us."

"It's to keep you from escaping." He took a step forward, as I took one back.

"Why does it feel like I'm prey and you're stalking me?"

He began to unbutton his shirt, and my throat dried up.

"Am I stalking you, Tara?" His shirt fell to the floor, revealing a soft cotton T-shirt.

I took another step in retreat as the need coursing down my pussy threatened to soak through my underwear.

The simple white shirt shouldn't have looked so appealing but on him, it did, revealing chiseled arms and a chest that one would never expect on a politician, broad and defined, perfect to hold on to.

Before I could reach out to touch him, the backs of my knees hit the baseboard of the bed, stopping my backward trek.

Ashur took hold of my ribcage. "I want you on the bed, but not just yet."

I swallowed at the intensity of his gaze.

His palms slowly slid upward until he reached my aching breasts. Then, instead of cupping them, he circled his thumbs along the tips, forcing my nipples into stiffer, harder peaks.

"That's better." He continued his lazy caress, and just when I was ready to ask for more, he pinched.

I cried out, letting the sting and the desire flow through every nerve in my body. I'd never thought I'd enjoy any pain with my pleasure, but with Ashur, it was a heady mix.

"Take off your clothes, Tara. I want to see you. I want to touch what is mine."

"Yours?"

"Yes, mine."

"What about you? Are you mine?"

Why had I asked him that?

"I've always been yours for over fifteen years. Time and distance never changed that."

"Ash, why do you say things like that? I don't know how to handle this."

"Let it happen. This time here is ours, Tara. Don't let the outside world interfere. Remember there is no past or anything beyond each other."

I studied him for a second. Could I risk it?

Who was I kidding? I was completely caught in his web and I couldn't think of anything better than to be with this man.

Stepping onto my tiptoes, I bit his bottom lip and said, "Okay. Here. In this cabin. There is only us."

He fisted a hand in my hair as he ate at my mouth.

"Now back to what I said before, get naked. I want to touch you."

I shifted out of his hold, giving him my back. He lifted the strands of my hair, laying them on one shoulder, and kissed the hollow at the base of my ear. He grasped the zipper of my dress and tugged down. The soft fabric slid to the floor, leaving me in only a bra, panties, and a pair of thigh-highs.

Goosebumps prickled my skin and I let out a low moan.

"Now this is unexpected." He traced the henna-style tattoo that ran from the back of my shoulder to the left curve of my bottom. "I don't remember seeing this before."

"That's because we were too desperate to fuck yesterday to even think about getting me naked."

"I remember that weekend at Jacinta's estate you wore a bikini." There was a ting of possessive irritation in his tone. "And it did very little to cover your assets."

I couldn't help but smile. "That weekend I wore a sheer cover-up in a similar pattern to my tattoo so you wouldn't have noticed."

Nearly two years ago, Ashur had crashed a weekend gathering at Jacinta's family estate. It was supposed to be my place to recover from the fallout of my work in the No Bride project. Jacinta and Samina had rallied around me and forced me to relax and recuperate. We'd barely spent an hour relaxing by the pool under the spring sun, when Ashur had shown up to join the festivities.

It was during that weekend I learned I wasn't truly over him.

Ashur followed the design in slow, soft glides of his fingers. "When did you get it?"

"Ten years ago." I hoped he wouldn't ask me why I'd gotten the ink or why I'd chosen the design.

If he knew I'd wanted the tattoo to feel closer to him after he'd gone missing while deployed, he'd know this was more than business between us. He'd know I'd...I wasn't ready to go there.

"It's beautiful. It reminds me of that drawing I made you when we went to Galveston for a picnic."

I kept quiet, just focusing on his touch and not his words. Galveston, Texas wasn't one of the prettiest beaches in the world, but for me it was a special place, reminding me of a time before I'd lost my innocence.

"Now face me and then take off your bra."

I followed his instructions, reaching behind me, unclasping my bra, and dropping it to the ground.

"God, you're fucking gorgeous."

His praise gave me a sense of happiness I hadn't expected.

"Cup your breasts. Offer them to me," he ordered.

Without thought I following his instructions, holding my large mounds in my palms and lifting my chest toward him. He bent his head and closed his lips around one taut nipple, biting the tip, in an exquisite pleasure-pain. The soft wet heat of him engulfed me as he rolled his tongue around the aching nub, laving it and teasing. Sensations shot through every nerve in my body.

I gasped, closing my eyes and throwing my head back.

He slipped a hand behind my back, leveraging me toward him, and repeated the delicious torture on the other breast. I gripped his shoulders, writhing in bliss.

When had my breasts become so sensitive? I was on the verge of coming. This had never happened to me before.

"So responsive. I knew you'd be this way."

"Ashur, what are you doing to me?"

"I'm making love to you, baby."

I opened my eyes and reached out to touch him, but he shook his head and stepped out of my reach.

"Ask."

I bit my lip. He'd been serious about the boss-in-the-bedroom thing. But wasn't that what had attracted me to him in the first place? His control, his dominance, his knowledge of what I needed.

"May I touch you?"

He pulled his white T-shirt over his head, revealing his perfect ink-covered torso and pecs.

Dear God. I wasn't the gorgeous one, he was.

Lifting my hand, he placed it over his heart. The heat of his skin seeped into my fingertips.

He stared into my eyes and the emotion I saw there destroyed me inside. "Do you want me, Tara?"

How could any sane woman not want him?

"Yes," I whispered.

"Good." He lifted his hand, freeing mine. "Touch me."

He wouldn't need to repeat himself. I ran my hand up his shoulder and alone his arms in feathered strokes. Up and down, letting my fingers memorize every plain and valley.

Goosebumps prickled his flesh, and it satisfied me to know he had the same reaction I had whenever any part of him connected with my body.

I stroked his pecs and abdomen, enjoying the quickening of his breath. I followed the winding tattoos covering the left side of his body. They were so intricate, so unique, so similar to the one covering my back. There was meaning behind all of it, one filled with history and pain, something I wouldn't bring up to mar the moment. I tried my best to ignore the slightly puckered skin hidden under the long tongue of a winding cobra but the need to comfort got the best of me and I kissed one of the long, jagged marks.

Ashur inhaled deep and clenched his fists at his sides.

Immediately I pulled back. "Am I hurting you?"

He cupped my face. "No, baby. I'm just sensitive there."

"Will you tell me about it one day?"

"Yes, but not tonight. Tonight is about us. Not the past."

I continued my exploration of his upper body, enjoying every little flinch of his muscles and the increased rhythm of his breath.

Just as I moved to cup his straining cock, he grabbed my wrist.

"No more petting. I want to fuck you. My cock has barely gone down since I watched you come apart in the lavatory, and any more of your gentle torture will drive me insane."

"Then fuck me, Ashu."

Ashur smiled, lifting me into his giant arms, and crawled onto the bed. He set me down with a gentleness that was a sharp contrast to the need radiating from him. Rolling to his side, he unfastened his buckle and pants. He pulled them down his long legs one at a time and then dumped them on the floor. He boxer briefs did nothing to hide the cock bulging against the cotton material. Next went his underwear, and he was there in all his naked glory. His cock glistened with pre-cum, curving past his belly button.

How he kept all that delicious manhood in his pants was a wonder.

I licked my lips. I couldn't wait until I got a taste of his velvety hard length in my mouth.

"Stop staring at my cock. I'm barely holding on as it is."

"I can't help myself." I came up on my arms. "I want to suck you off."

He groaned. "Not helping. Next time."

He came toward me, grasping my ankles and tugging me in his direction. He took hold of my underwear and ripped it from my body, making me gasp.

He spread my thighs, opening me to his heated gaze. His arousal spurred mine. I cupped my breasts to ease my need but all it did was make me crave him more.

He rolled his cock up and down my cleft, mixing our juices together. The engorged head of his erection rimmed my weeping pussy. I lifted my hips to engulf him but Ashur held me in place.

"I say when I fuck you. If I tell you to wait, then you wait. From this moment, I own your pleasure. No getting yourself off unless I give you permission."

He rubbed his cock up my folds again, circling my swollen, sensitive clit.

My back bowed and I growled. "Ashu, please."

"Do I make myself clear, Tara? Do you accept every moan, every contraction of your pussy belongs to me?"

"Yes. I belong to you. No one but you."

He slammed into me and immediately my mind clouded with an insatiable need to come, and a guttural cry of desperate hunger escaped from my mouth.

Ashur's knee dipped onto the bed and his weight and

body surrounded me. I wrapped my legs around his waist, tilting my hips to meet each thrust.

My nails dug into his back, and he let out a hiss. The next thing I knew, he'd captured my arms and pinned them above my head in the tight grip of one palm.

He loomed over me, panting and pounding in my aching core. We kissed as he thrust, letting our bodies slide against each other.

He kept a hard, steady pace that had me shattering moments later. I convulsed and contracted around him. Clenching my eyes tight, I reveled in the intensity of my release.

My focus had barely returned before he brought me up again.

For a man who was supposedly hanging on by a thread, he had impeccable control. I orgasmed another two times, and with the last one he followed, calling out my name and pumping his hot cum deep inside me.

CHAPTER FOURTEEN

I stepped into the kitchen of the cabin, a little before seven in the morning. No matter how exhausted I was or how hard I'd tried, I couldn't sleep. Maybe it was all the craziness of past forty-eight hours keeping my mind active. Or the fact that a sexy-as-sin man slept in my bed. Whatever it was, I had to get my ass up when I'd started counting the chirps of the birds outside my window in hopes of lulling myself to sleep.

Tightening my robe over my naked body, I stepped farther into the room. A yawn escaped my lips and I lifted my arms and stretched high, trying to release some of the aches in my body. My muscles were sore, but it was a good kind of sore. Ones achieved from four rounds of bone-melting sex.

Last night, Ashur had taken me as a man who knew what he wanted and how to get it. The sex wasn't the innocent-and-gentle lovemaking I'd had with him when we were oh-so young, but all-consuming and filled with a passion and dominance I'd never experienced before.

I gripped the counter near a set of windows and licked my lips as a slow hum began to beat deep inside me.

Seriously, Tara. Get a hold of yourself. You've gone years without needing sex and now you've become a fucking nymphomaniac. Stop thinking about his cock. You're the first lady, for God's sake. Keep your shit together!

I shook my reprimand from my head and gazed out the window toward the Colorado River. Birds flew about, and their feathers shone brightly against the glow of the sunrise. Two deer raced past the fenced yard of the cottage's gardens, jumping over the bushes without a single pause.

God. Never in a million years would I have thought I'd spend my honeymoon in a remote cabin, albeit a very large one, in the woods near Austin, Texas.

I was the furthest thing from outdoorsy. White sand beach, swimming in the turquoise water, and sipping cocktails was more up my alley.

But there was a beauty to this area I'd never appreciated in all the years I'd lived in Texas. I felt a sense of peacefulness, something I hadn't experienced since...I paused, thinking about when I'd last felt calm or peaceful. Had it been so long that I couldn't remember?

Well, shit. Ashur had fucked my brains out enough to

allow me to enjoy woodsy nature. What was the world coming to?

We'd always been opposites. Where he enjoyed camping, I loved a spa. I was high fashion and he was sports and outdoors. And then there was his obsession with high-end scotch, whereas give me a bold Brunello, and I was in heaven.

One of the few topics we agreed on was our mutual love for all things meat. Give us a juicy filet and we were in heaven. It probably had to do with the fact both of us were Texans.

I wasn't sure how long I stood at the counter gazing out the window, but I moved when my stomach made a very un-first-ladylike rumble.

I glanced at the phone on the wall and then decided against calling the compound staff to bring breakfast.

For years, I'd cooked for myself, and it wasn't as if I'd forgotten how to feed myself, even with all the fancy dinners and galas of the past two years. Besides, it was something I enjoyed wholeheartedly. No one would ever think that hardnosed, take-no-one's-shit, human-rights attorney Tara Zain...em...Tara Kumar would enjoy watching cooking shows and making the delicious meals she saw on television during her alone time.

Maybe Ash still remembered.

For the short summer we'd been together all those years ago, I'd made many a dish for him to try. Some had failed epically and others had come out phenomenal successes. I'd remembered how Ashur had complained he was going to gain too much weight, all the while stuffing his mouth.

I sighed. What had happened to that sweet and thoughtful man? I couldn't have been the cause of him becoming so hard or the asshole as he'd like to call himself.

Then a vision of the tattoo-covered scars that ran along his abdomen and shoulder came to mind, and I knew it probably had more to do with all that he'd experienced during his tours in the military.

I knew I'd been the reason he'd joined the military. He was trying to escape the memories of me, and because of me, he had nearly died.

I flinched inside. I couldn't go there.

I walked to the satellite radio console and selected a station. I needed some old-school hip-hop to keep my mind from thinking too hard. As I selected my station, I smiled and began to sing along. There was nothing like 90's Salt-N-Pepa.

Ameera and I used to dance around our apartment when we were between assignments to let off steam. We had an eclectic taste in music that had no rhyme or reason. Our only steadfast rule was that whoever chose the music had to start the dance-off.

God, I missed her. Soon. I'd see her and then deal with whatever the future held for both of us.

You hang on, Ame. If I have to bring you back myself, I'll get you home. I won't ever give up.

As the music kicked on, I refocused on the task of making breakfast. I searched the pantry and cabinets, gathering all the ingredients to make hazelnut chocolate French toast, something I knew Ashur enjoyed. Samina had told me that she was so glad I taught her how to make the breakfast indulgence. Especially since Ashur would require her to make the dish whenever he visited her in Seattle.

Setting each item on the island, I pulled out the mixing bowl and created an eggy batter with the right amount of vanilla and cinnamon for the gourmet bread I'd use to concoct my masterpiece.

I danced around the room, gyrating my hips and rapping the lyrics of "Push It." After a few minutes of trying to imitate the moves from the 90's videos, I scooped out a hefty serving of hazelnut spread into a glass container.

Taking the spoon out of the chocolate, I stuck it in my mouth and moaned. This was heaven. I reached for the frying pan and jumped.

A bare-chested, impeccably chiseled Ashur, wearing only a pair of low-lying pajama pants leaned against the doorjamb, watching me with an intensity that made my already rapid heartbeat jump to an even faster rhythm.

"Don't stop on my account. The cooking show is spectacular."

"Ashur," I gasped, pulling the spoon out of my mouth. "How long have you been there?

A smile tugged his lips. "Long enough."

I felt the heat creeping up my body and setting like flames over my cheeks.

"Still love 90's hip-hop, I see."

He rose from his perch on the wall and walked toward me.

"What's not to love? It's fun and makes a girl want to dance." I backed up as he advanced, and I found myself caged between the island and Ashur's hard body.

He plucked the spoon from my hand and glanced at the bowls on the counter. "Were you making French toast for me?"

"Maybe." I pressed my fingers to his chest, watching him warily.

He gazed into my eyes with a soft look and then said, "Thank you. Sam tries but she never could make it the way you did."

"Want to do this with me? This way you can make it whenever the mood hits." I tried to duck under his arm, but he crowded me against the counter.

"No. I'd rather do something else." He lifted the spoon he held, dipped it in the container of hazelnut spread, and then ran it down the slope of my throat before dropping it back into the bowl.

"Like what?" I asked, feeling arousal pulse to life inside me.

His bent his neck and then licked along the path the chocolate coated my skin. I let out a moan and arched into his touch.

He lifted me onto the counter, pushing all the bowls and utensils to the other side of the island.

"Like have my breakfast."

Ashur untied the belt holding my robe closed, pushing it off my shoulders and exposing my naked body underneath. The fabric pooled at my arms, but when I moved to free my hand, Ashur shook his head.

"Leave them right there." A wicked gleam entered his gaze that made my pussy flood with desire. "Now flatten your palms. I don't want you falling."

"What are you going to do if I move?"

He reached over and grabbed the container of the hazelnut spread next to me.

"It's simple. I won't let you come."

I lifted my chin. "I don't need you to make me come."

"Yes, you do, Tara." His voice grew gruff and he brought his face a hairsbreadth from mine. "Your orgasms belong me and I won't share. The only time your hand gets to pleasure your body is if I'm watching."

His words had my core clenching as my nipples beaded to hard points.

"I see the idea appeals to you." He pulled back and stirred the contents of the bowl with the spoon.

I licked my parched lips, focusing on the tented front of his pajama bottoms and said, "As it does for you."

My breath was coming out in short pants, and goosebumps prickled my flesh. I felt the urge to slide off the counter, coat his cock in the spread, and blow his mind.

I jumped as a cool droplet of chocolate drizzled onto my shoulder, making my attention return to Ashur.

"You're going to make me sticky."

Another glob of hazelnut fell into the valley of my breasts and over my nipples and down to my glistening sex. "That's the point. I want you sticky, wet, sweaty, writhing under me, and begging me to let you come."

"Ashu, are you going to keep talking or are you going to do something?"

Ashur growled, dropped the container and spoon onto the counter with a sharp rattle, and cupped my chocolate-covered breasts. He massaged the mounds and then pinched the tips as he brought his mouth down to nip the buds with his teeth.

I cried out as he engulfed a nipple in his mouth.

"Does this answer your question?" he murmured as he moved to the other breast. "Now be a good girl and let me enjoy my morning wakeup."

He flicked and swirled his tongue, lapping at the sugary concoction and making my clit throb for the attention he was levying on my breasts.

I gasped and bowed as he feasted on my breasts and upper body. By the time he licked down my stomach, I was on the verge of coming, and he hadn't even grazed my clit.

"Ashu—" my body was on fire, "—I need you to make me come."

"Sorry, love, but you moved your hands."

Instantly, I realized my fingers were clutched in his hair and I'd been using his head as leverage to keep me from falling backward. I released my hold on him and gripped the edge of the granite.

He looked up my body and smiled against my abdomen.

He held my gaze as his chocolate-covered tongue dipped into my bellybutton and then trailed to the swollen folds of my labia.

Spreading my thighs apart, his attention moved to my soaked sex. He circled the sensitive bundle of nerves of my clit three times before spearing deep into my sopping pussy. He ate me like a man starved, bringing me to the edge of orgasm too many times to count.

"Please," I whimpered, throwing my head back. Tears rimmed my eyes as my need was to the point I wouldn't be able to go on any longer without release. "I can't take it anymore."

"I know, baby. I won't make you wait any longer." He rose to his feet, pulling me to the edge of the counter.

He cupped my face, thumbing the tears of frustration dampening my cheeks, and kissed me hard and with a passion that had my head reeling.

"Do you want me?"

"Dammit, Ashu. I never stopped wanting you."

"I know. I just needed to hear you say it."

Reaching between our bodies, he pushed down his pants and freed his thick, hard cock. He positioned himself at my entrance and slammed in to the hilt.

We both cried out at the same time.

"How is it you're so tight? I've fucked you six times in less than two days." He pulled out and hammered back in.

"Why are you asking me stupid questions? I need to come. Will you fuck me already?" I bit his shoulder but kept my hands on the island.

The sadistic bastard would probably stop if I moved them.

"Sheathe the fangs. I'll make it good for you."

Ashur fisted my hair with his fingers and gripped my hip tight, ensuring I'd probably have another bruise or two to add to the ones Casey gave me from sparring. Then he set a hard, unrelenting pounding that had me sliding up the stone counter to only be brought back again to meet his thrust.

Th friction ignited the almost painful ache Ashur had

stirred and I erupted, bowing my back as my hard nipples scraped against his chest.

Sensations of falling filled my mind and my pussy clamped down on his pistoning cock.

Just as I was coming down, Ashur changed his pace and my need started again. He made me come one more time before he let go and collapsed against me on the granite.

***

"DAMN. THIS IS INCREDIBLE."

I shook my head at Ashur as he inhaled his sixth piece of French toast. The way he was eating it was a wonder his body was still so rock hard.

"Want me to make another batch? I have the ends of the loaf left."

He looked up from his plate. "Are you saying I'm eating like a pig?"

"Oink, oink."

He picked up my plate and set it in front of him. And then preceded to eat again.

I gawked at him.

He looked up. "What? Fucking you senseless worked up an appetite. I need my energy if I'm to keep up with a wife who is five years younger than me and has an insatiable need for my cock."

"If you want to use me as an excuse, go right ahead."

He gave me his heart-stopping grin. "Can I use that excuse when I want a blow job in my office between meetings?"

"You're incorrigible."

"Yes, but it still doesn't take away from the fantasy of having my wife sucking my cock in the middle of the Oval Office."

"Not going to happen." I scrunched up my face in exaggerated disgust. "A distant predecessor of yours already took that idea."

Ashur used the last piece of French toast to sop up the maple syrup before bringing it to his mouth. He licked his lips and hummed.

How did a man make eating a kid's breakfast look so damn sexy doing it?

"Want to go for a run?" Ashur said, as he pushed back from the table.

Glancing toward the Secret Service agents patrolling the grounds outside the giant bay window of the breakfast nook, I said, "Are we allowed to leave the cabin?"

"Tara, I own this property, including the land. We aren't prisoners, we just happened to be two people who require a lot of security."

"Won't it cause a logistics nightmare for Jake and the rest of the Secret Service agents?"

"They know the drill. It would surprise them more if I

holed up inside the cabin. I'm known for my runs in the middle of winter, with snow and ice on the ground."

"Yeah, you are a bit obsessed with running. I'll stick with martial arts and yoga. The only reason my ass gets out to run is because my trainer makes me do it as part of my required bi-weekly training sessions."

Fuck, why'd I say that?

He studied me for a moment, and I held my breath. *Please don't have picked up on the last thing I said.*

"I'm sure I could get you to enjoy runs."

I nearly sighed in relief.

"The only way I'd enjoy long runs was if there was a giant piece of chocolate cake waiting for me at the end as a reward."

"Would a bout of hot, sticky, raunchy sex do?"

My pulse jumped.

He laughed, reached over to cup the back of my head, and planted a hard kiss on my lips.

"Like I said, insatiable."

"Ashur?" I murmured, pulling back a bit and staring into his eyes.

"Yes."

"I love being here like this. It's simple and..." I paused. "I'm not sure how to say this. It's easy. Does that make sense?"

"Yes, it does." He rested his forehead against mine.

"You don't have to always be on guard with me. You can talk to me."

Tears burned the backs of my eyes.

"I want to. I've never had anyone to truly share things with, but I'm worried that once you know my secrets, you'll..." I trailed off, turning my head away.

"You can trust me." He tilted my chin up. "Tara, we all have secrets. Yours can't be any worse than mine."

"I'm not squeaky clean like you are. I don't do the right thing even if it will cost me."

"You think I don't know that you've circumvented numerous international laws in your pro-bono work? Honestly, I'm impressed no one besides Edgar ever challenged you on it."

"I'm a liability to you."

"I'll worry about that. Your need to protect and fight for the underdog is what has endeared you to so many around the world. Although, I'd appreciate if you would refrain from joining any underground organizations of crazy crusaders until I'm out of office."

I winced inside. Oh boy. I was up shit creek. The plans to get Ameera back were as crazy and vigilante as they got.

He must have noticed my reaction to his words. "Tara, trust me. I trust you."

Trusting him was something I never thought I could do. Now I wanted to so desperately confide in him, find comfort in him, to know that he would still be there in the end.

"I'll try," I whispered.

"That's all I can ask. I'll fight for you, T-Rex."

My heart skipped a beat. He'd said the one thing that would put a crack in my defenses against him.

"I swear I'm going to kick Tyler's ass," I muttered. "Why do you call me that? You don't even know why he gave me the name."

"I know. It's because you are tiny, with little arms, but could bite anyone's head off if they got in the way of your causes."

"I'll show you tiny arms." My fist flew out to punch his shoulder, but he caught it in the palm of his hand.

"Fast, but not fast enough, young Padawan."

"Young Padawan, my ass. My days as an apprentice are long behind me. I'm a full-fledged Jedi Master." I beamed at him.

And here was another thing we had in common. Our mutual, geeky love of all things *Star Wars*.

"Come on." He ran a thumb over my knuckle. "Let's see if you can keep up with this old man. For the next few hours, it's just you, me, and nature."

I turned up my nose at the last word of his sentence, which resulted in an eye roll from Ashur.

Ashur stood, scooping me up and then throwing me over his shoulder.

I screamed. "What are you doing? Put me down."

"To change. We're going to go for a run, and the hell if I'm going to let anyone see you in a bathrobe, Jedi Master or not."

"You really are a Neanderthal as Tyler said, Mr. Kumar."

"Never denied it, Mrs. Kumar."

CHAPTER FIFTEEN

I groaned inside as I adjusted my pillow for what felt like the hundredth time. For over an hour, I'd tried to sleep but nothing worked. It was still pitch-black outside and even the annoying birds were sleeping. Which meant, I couldn't use them as my excuse for the insomnia I was going through. I covered my face with my arm and released a deep breath.

There was no use in pretending I had no clue what was bothering me. We'd leave for Washington after breakfast and I couldn't help but worry what it would be like between us when we took on our roles as president and first lady and not just a man and woman totally into each other.

Would we live separate lives and only come together for sex and the occasional event or would we have a relationship as my parents had? One where we shared everything that wasn't confidential to our jobs.

My emotions were running wild, and the need I felt for Ashur was confusing the hell out of me.

These past few days he'd been the boy I'd fallen in love with as a girl but in the package of the man he'd become. He'd gotten me to enjoy our early-morning walks and late-night strolls. Although he hadn't proven to me running was worth it. We'd even broached the subject of his father, discussing in detail Minesh's manipulation and even what he'd done to Samina when she'd decided to pursue a career far away from Texas.

I'd found myself wanting to confess everything about who I was and what I'd done, countless times. But I'd kept things quiet, not wanting anything to taint our time at the cabin. Plus, it was better to have all the information and then tell Ashur everything. As soon as we got back, I'd meet with Tyler, settle on the final logistics of the auction and Ameera's return, and then decide how I'd talk to Ashur.

I had no doubt Ashur would keep my secret. It was better that he knew so he could head off any future fallout.

I sighed.

I'd have to wait and see if he could accept who I was. Who I work for...who I worked for.

God, how was I going to give up the job that had given me my identity? I still had four months to change my mind.

Fuck, there was no way this couldn't end in disaster.

Then there was the contract. It was my safety net in my relationship with Ashur. He'd offered the money and I'd accepted it. But now, especially after this week, I could see us truly making this a real marriage.

Would it be as simple as saying I wanted to tear up the contract?

What if I took the step and he turned his back on me when he learned about Solon? Ashur said he knew I'd hedged international law and accepted what I'd done as a way to save lives and to protect the innocent.

But would he feel the same when he learned that there was no hedging, I'd broken nearly every law of every country when it came to engaging with negotiating with terrorists and had no guilt whatsoever in doing it.

His whole election platform had been about doing the right thing, making decisions within the confines of the law and procedure, and working across party lines. He viewed vigilantism as undermining government stability. I couldn't blame his views on his military career. He'd thought this way when I'd first met him. He'd always say, "If you don't like the way things are run, then vote them out or work to pass new laws."

The fact I'd engaged in espionage would be a hard pill for him to swallow.

He'd chiseled away so much of the protection I'd had

surrounding my heart that I wasn't sure I could handle his rejection.

Maybe it was better to focus on living out the terms of the agreement rather than risk giving him my love and having him turn his back on it.

Who are you kidding? He's held your heart since you were eighteen. No wall you erect around our emotions will change how you feel about him.

Turning to my side, I looked at Ashur and caught him watching me.

"What are you thinking about so hard?" he asked.

No way was I going to tell him. I was feeling raw enough.

"Sorry. I didn't mean to wake you."

"I couldn't sleep either."

He moved over to me, caging me with his giant arms.

"Stop worrying. We're married. We'll figure out the details as we go. I'm sure this first lady thing will be a breeze compared to your pro-bono work."

And then there was the other thing I'd tried to forget over the last week.

My new role.

"Wrong, I'd rather deal with the hell of international litigation." I set my hand on his shoulder. "I don't know how to be the first lady. All I know is me."

He leaned down until we were nose to nose. "You are the one I want. The woman who made something of herself on her terms. The woman who commands respect because she isn't afraid to face off against the scariest motherfuckers in the world to protect an innocent child."

"You say this now, but you may not feel the same when you learn everything I've done."

"Do you really think I'm so innocent? When my plane went down in North Africa, do you really think I was there for a joy ride?"

I'd heard rumors over the years that Ashur and Veer had been spying for the government when their plane was shot down by a rebel group in South Sudan.

"You weren't breaking American law. You were following orders."

"Tara, you're too good of a lawyer to break any law to a level you can't talk your way out of."

I almost grimaced. He viewed me in a way I never deserved. It would have been so much easier if he'd never wanted more from me and kept the business-only plan we'd agreed to in the beginning.

"Stop worrying. Have you not figured it out? I lo—"

I lifted my mouth to his, cutting off his words. He was tying me in knots, and if he said the words, I'd lose myself even more than I already had.

But he pulled back, pinning my arms above my head with one of his as he tugged my thighs apart and settled his naked body between my legs.

"I wasn't finished." He loomed over me, his gaze both sleepy and intense.

"Please, Ashu. Don't." A tear slipped past my eye.

"I get you aren't ready to hear it but it doesn't change how I feel."

The tip of his cock slid along my dampening cleft.

"Why are you saying this? We have an agreement."

He pushed into my swollen pussy, making me gasp and arch against his hard thrust.

"A piece of paper doesn't change the fact we've always wanted each other." He pulled out and slammed back in. "That what we felt for each other has never changed."

Before I could retort he spoke again. "Don't even think about denying this thing between us. This is more than sex, more than making a baby. It is more."

"Why won't you leave it alone?" I tried to tug my hands free, which only intensified his hold on my wrist and the pace of his cock pounding into me.

My body responded and a spasm shot through my core, contracting around his cock.

"Because I never skim over the truth, and the truth is that you belong to me."

Ashur continued to stare into my eyes as he held my hip with each drive of his cock.

I couldn't look away and I knew he saw how I felt. How I needed him. How lost I was in him.

"Ashu, please," I whispered. And I wasn't sure what I

begged for, my orgasm or an end to the emotions he stirred in me.

As my body teetered on the cusp of release, my heart told me I'd only have him for a limited time. He saw so much in black and white, wrong and right. And I was a hodgepodge mixture of a technicolor rainbow.

If it came down to choosing between following the rules and breaking every law to get Ameera back, I'd do it in a heartbeat.

Another tear slid past my lids.

"Look at me." Ashur bit my lower lip, bringing my focus to him. "This is us. Don't ever forget what we are to each other."

He cupped my breast, rolling the tip with his fingers, and then pinched the sensitive nub.

My gaze clouded as the pleasure-pain sent me over, and my release washed over me, back bowing and pussy squeezing in waves around his girth.

"You're mine, Tara. You were always mine."

"Yes," I answered, digging my heels into the back of his thighs. "As long as you want me."

"Forever." He pulled out to the tip and then slammed into my spasming pussy. "No other woman holds a candle to you."

Ashur's pace grew unsteady and a few moments later he came in hard spurts.

"Hi Leara," I said as I entered the area leading to the Oval Office. "Is the meeting over?"

"Yes. You can go right in."

I smiled and took the short hallway to the Oval Office.

The second Ashur and I had stepped through the doorway of the White House, Ashur was bombarded with requests and issues that required his immediate attention. One of them being a last-minute trade summit in Oslo that he'd have to leave for in two days' time.

There went the hope we'd get to ease into our marriage and our roles.

Now it was four hours later and I had no idea what to do. I'd unpacked, explored, officially meet all the White House staff as first lady, and checked in to make sure everything was still on target for Ameera's auction.

If only I had a pile of briefs to keep me occupied. No matter how much I dreaded the time-consuming task of reviewing case files, at least it would keep me occupied and not roaming the halls of the White House.

What the hell had I just thought? I was on a mission to become un-bored by seducing my husband.

I paused outside the door and waited until the guards opened it for me to walk through and then closed it behind me.

Ashur looked up from the papers he was reading and smiled.

My heart immediately skipped a beat. He was so handsome, and when he smiled it was breathtaking.

"Hello there, First Lady."

"How's it going, Mr. President?"

"Much better now that you're here." He stood and came around his desk. "Tell me not to go and I'll stay here."

"I can't do that." I shook my head. "You've wanted this summit for the past year. This is your opportunity to fix the relationships your predecessor destroyed."

"I take it your dislike for Edgar hasn't eased?"

Lifting a brow, I flicked Ashur's tie with my fingers. "The only redeeming quality about that man is his wife. It will take two terms for you to undo half the shit that man did to this country."

"Not everything he did while in office was bad."

Furrowing my brow, I scowled. "He negated anything redeemable about him the day he said the American people had better things to do then worry about immigrant girls in another country whether they were forced to marry an older man or not."

I remembered the first time the recording of Edgar discussing the captured American girls had leaked to the press. It still made me sick to think about. The audio file revealed Edgar had a tier for whom he considered to be an American citizen. He'd had the nerve to say that since those girls were the first generations born in the US, their value wasn't as important as those who'd lived here for multiple generations.

I couldn't wait until the day the bastard keeled over, then the world and sweet Amanda Edgar would be free of the asshole.

"Woo, Tiger. I see the fire burning in those eyes. Forget I said anything positive about him." He slid an arm around my waist, drawing me to him and giving me a wicked grin.

I released a deep breath. "You riled me up on purpose."

"What can I say? I love it when my wife gets in her 'save the world from the pseudo-dictator' mode."

"I hope you remember this statement when I give you grief with my many crusades."

"I think I can handle it." As he said those words, his gaze softened and filled with an emotion I still couldn't get used to seeing or accepting.

I hadn't let him say the words on our honeymoon, but I knew how he felt.

I wanted to hear them, to accept them, to believe this thing between us would last beyond the contract, but would he still feel the same about me once he learned all the things I'd done and was still doing to undermine the laws he worked to uphold?

"Stop thinking, Tara. Accept what we are."

"I do accept us." I glanced to the side, not wanting him to see the uncertainty I felt.

He cupped my nape and pressed a thumb up the column of my throat until my chin was tilted so I could look into his eyes.

"No, baby. You want to trust in us but you fear it won't last. I've told you. I'll fight for us."

"Ash." I stood on tiptoes. "Don't make promises you may not be able to keep."

I covered his mouth with my fingers before he could argue. We stared at each other for a few seconds.

I wasn't supposed to let it get to this level of emotion ever again. I should have protected myself. Hell, I should have protected him. I was going to destroy this man once again with deceit, but this time with was my own doing, not because someone else was forcing me to do it.

Ashur pulled my hand away and said, "You think too much, Mrs. Kumar. I believe I need to occupy your mind with something more important." Then he sealed his lips against mine.

I let out a slow moan as his intoxicating taste invaded my mouth. He deepened the kiss, pushing his tongue past my lips and igniting my desire for him. All my worries and uncertainty were replaced by a lust-filled need.

He lifted me against him and maneuvered us until he reached the sofa in the far corner and sat down with me on top of him without breaking our embrace.

"I want to do something," I murmured while continuing to nip on his soft lips.

"What?"

Sliding off him, I dropped to the floor between his legs. Slowly, I glided my hands up his thighs, feeling the muscles bunch as my fingers crept closer to his engorged erection.

Leaning down, I nuzzled the line of his cock behind the fabric of his pants.

"Tara, I thought you said this has been done."

Was that panic and uncertainty in his voice?

Oh. Mr. President was anxious about the cameras. A sense of power flooded my system, and I wanted to see how far he'd let me go.

"I changed my mind. This isn't something illicit. Besides—" I unbuckled his belt and then lowered his zipper, "—it's my husband's fantasy to have me on my knees in his office, sucking his cock."

"There is something to be said when a fantasy becomes a reality." He watched me with a devilish grin.

"Does this mean you're going to let me have my wicked way with you in the office?"

"Absolutely, Mrs. Kumar. Especially since I turned off the surveillance when you came in."

"So, you were expecting something scandalous to occur?"

"I knew it was a distinct possibility. You see, my wife craves my cock as much as I crave her pussy."

Heat and desire sizzled through core. I couldn't figure out why, but I loved it when he was crude and unrefined with his words.

His fingers slipped into my hair as I tugged at the waistband of his pants, pulling his shirt free and giving me access to his boxer briefs. The beautiful thick, hard length of his cock strained against the snub cotton, and with a slight shift of the fabric, it bobbed free, a hairsbreadth from my salivating mouth.

A man's erection wasn't supposed to be so appealing, so arousing, so tempting.

My tongue poked out, licking the drop of precum on his flared head before circling the crown three times. I gripped the back of his cock and then trailed the line from his sac to the weeping slit at the tip of his length, dipping my tongue into the ridge.

He let out a small hiss and tightened his hold in my hair.

He tilted my head back and gazed down at me with lust and need. "Open up, love. I want my cock to imprint itself into the back of your throat."

"As you wish." I opened my lips and he pushed in deep.

I had to immediately relax and swallow to open the back of my mouth and not to choke on his generous length.

A moan escaped his lips. "Yes, baby. That's it. Fuck. I love that mouth of yours."

I began a slow and steady rhythm. Moving up and down and following each stroke of my mouth with a squeeze in the same direction as my palm.

I pressed my thighs together, trying to alleviate some of my own need pulsing in my pussy.

He grabbed hold of my hair, moving it out of the way so he could watch me work his cock. "I love watching your lips as my cock fucks into your hot, wet mouth. It's almost as good as your cunt."

A shiver worked its way across my body and I had to touch myself. As I worked him, I pushed the finger of my free hand past the waistband of my pants and underwear through my soaked slit and to my aching clit.

A spasm shot through me, causing me to lose the tempo of my mouth on Ashur's throbbing cock.

He immediately tugged my mouth off him with a hard jerk that had me gasping for air and crying out with an insatiable need to continue.

He glared down his body. "Did you forget, unless I give you permission, you don't get to make yourself come? Your orgasms belong to me."

I stopped the motion of my fingers. My eyes watered, desperate for the orgasm that was almost on me.

"Please, Ashu." I moaned.

"Come here."

I released his cock, pulled my hands from my pussy, and moved up his body. Before I knew what was happening, I found myself face forward against the back of the couch with Ashur behind me. He unfastened my pants, shoved them down, and impaled me on his cock. I cried out, arching against him.

He set a hard, fast pace that left me breathless and mindless. Within a few strokes I was going over and barely a two seconds later, Ashur followed.

"Excuse me, Mrs. Kumar."

I turned to Casey. There was a look in his eyes that had the hairs on the back of my neck standing up.

"May I have a word with you?" He glanced toward the guards stationed at the door.

"Sure. Leo, Aston, would you mind closing the door?"

They nodded and left me alone with Casey.

The second the click of the lock engaged, Casey spoke. "Before I begin, I am going to say I highly advise you against doing anything rash."

I frowned. "You do realize that only means you already know how I'm going to react?"

"Yes. I trained you."

"Not sure what that has to do with anything, but go ahead. What's going on?"

"Kartik Khan believes he's located the holding spot for

Ms. Kamini." Casey passed me surveillance images and a map. He pointed to an area about a two hours' drive north of Karachi, Pakistan. "There has been intense movement along the roads in this area, and locals have mentioned a blond-haired Caucasian woman living in the mountains."

"That section of the mountains is controlled by Fahad Awan. He's into arms, not human trafficking."

"It looks like he's decided to diversify." Casey showed me a few more images of Awan moving trucks filled with women and children into the area he controlled. "Kartik's sources say Awan is looking to unload a special package for the right price."

"Ameera."

Casey nodded. "I think our constant surveillance is taxing his resources. Plus, with a third-party interest in the auction, it only means there is a greater risk for him to be discovered."

"What are you saying?"

"Awan wants to meet with us. He says he's willing to trade his American package for double what his original buyer was willing to pay."

"When does Awan want to meet?"

"In two days' time."

"Then I guess I'm going to Pakistan." I pushed my rolling chair back and stood.

"I need to express my concern for you leaving while

the president is at the summit. There's no way to guarantee your safety."

"Your concern is noted. This is the first solid opportunity to get Ame back. I'll be damned if I'm going to wait around anymore. Get the plans in motion. We'll leave in two hours."

A LITTLE BEFORE FOUR FORTY-FIVE IN THE MORNING, my flight touched down at a remote landing strip an hour and a half north of Karachi, near the Hub Dam Wildlife Sanctuary. The property we were using as base camp was owned by Kartik Khan, a retired agent who happened to be part of one of the more influential families in Pakistan. His frequent travel schedule made it easy for access to and from his estate without drawing undue attention.

It had been two years since I last stepped foot on this property for my mission to save the American girls and nothing had changed. Sitting alongside the runway were a series of bunkers, and a fortified metal fence stretched for as far as the eye could see.

The area looked deceptively rural and barren but behind the façade was a military compound protected with the latest technology. Kartik liked to say no one could sneeze on his one hundred thousand acres without him knowing about it. He'd grown up looking over his shoulder so it made sense he wanted a safe place to call his own.

I gathered my day backpack, throwing it over my shoulder, and glanced at the two men Casey had assigned as my protection. They were both Solon agents who worked for the Secret Service.

"Is everything ready?" I asked Kartik the second I deplaned.

He handed me a map. "They are holding her here." He pointed to a bright-yellow-circled section of a small village near his estate. "There is a compound hidden near the cliffed section of the mountains. We believe she's in there. Awan and a group of his men were spotted leaving the area with their convoy about fifteen minutes before you touched down."

"How many do they have in the compound?"

"Our best guess is around twenty. He also left his best general behind."

Awan was known for keeping his top men with him at all times. If he left a general to oversee his territory, that meant he was leaving something very valuable behind.

Ameera.

"Where am I supposed to meet him?"

"I've arranged for a meeting at noon today at a café near Frere Hall in Karachi. Your decoy will check into the hotel near there in—" he glanced at his watch, "—exactly two hours and twenty-three minutes."

"Good. Make sure she doesn't leave the hotel until right before the meeting. This will give us approximately six hours to maneuver up the mountain, get into the compound, free Ame and get back here." I motioned for my protection to follow the other agents prepping for the mission and then strode toward the bunker that led to an underground tunnel into the main house of Kartik's mansion. "I'll need twenty minutes to freshen up and then we leave."

Kartik followed after me and said, "You can't go in. I won't risk you."

I stopped and turned a glare at him. "What's that supposed to mean?"

"If anything happened to you, I could never look Ashur in the eyes again. I've known him for longer than you have. That man loves you."

I'd forgotten Ashur and Kartik had met while studying at Harvard. They'd been part of a group of students who'd joined together to create a bitcoin farm. By the time they were in their senior year, all of their group had amassed such a high valuation of bitcoin that they were essentially billionaires. Thankfully they'd gotten out of the market before the bust and bought real estate in exchange for the high dollar value of their bitcoins.

"My relationship with Ashur has nothing to do with getting Ameera back." I scanned my eye against the bunker entrance and walked through, once it activated.

"It has everything to do with it. I was there the day the air force medevac brought him and Veer back to Germany after they'd gone missing. Ash thought he was going to die, and he didn't ask for his parents or his sister. He asked for you. He wanted to see you."

My steps faltered, and I braced my hand on a near wall.

He asked for me.

"Then why didn't anyone contact me?"

I knew the answer as soon as I asked the question.

"Minesh Kumar," was all Kartik said.

Minesh had tried to keep Samina from Ashur, so why would he allow me to see him?

My stomach hurt. All those times Ashur had said he'd never stopped wanting me or that he'd waited years to get me back, he wasn't just saying those things. He'd meant every word.

"I can't tell you how to handle any assignment, but I can voice my objection. If anything happened to you, it could cause more problems than anyone could ever imagine. No one outside of Solon knows you aren't in the US. Will you not consider coordinating from the trucks and let your team go in to get Ameera? She'd be the first to tell you not to come in guns blazing."

"I've never stood by while my team was in the line of fire. How can you expect me to watch from the sidelines?"

"You aren't only valuable to the men and women who

you lead. You belong to Ashur and your country. Your loyalty can't exclusively belong to Solon or your causes."

I almost denied his admonishment, but then stopped.

He was right.

For so many years, Solon and my law practice were all I had. My identity was tied to my role, to the lives I saved, to the innocent people I defended. My safety was a mild concern compared to those I saved from human trafficking.

Oh God, what had I done? I let my worry about Ameera cloud my judgment and put myself in a position that could not only destroy Ashur personally but also his position as president if it got out.

I glanced at Kartik, who watched me with knowing eyes. As if he'd had to make the same realization I'd just come to.

He gestured to the hallway and then said, "It isn't easy, but sometimes it's worth letting others take the lead if it means protecting the ones you love."

"Is that why you retired?"

Kartik had been one of the top agents in Solon. He was a legend. The countless lives he'd saved was a goal all of us had aspired to reach. Then one day, I was sent a report that Kartik had resigned from active duty status and would only work in a limited capacity of his choosing.

"I had to learn from my mistakes. The exact ones you are making."

"What do you mean?"

"Do you remember when I had my accident?"

"How could I forget? Tyler and I were the ones who found your shot-up car." I ducked under a low-hanging electrical wire and made my way to the door leading to the main house, but before I pushed it open I waited for Kartik's answer.

Whatever he had to say wasn't for anyone but us.

"I loved what I did for Solon. It gave me a purpose, but while I was getting my next fix of adventure—" his face grew grim, "—I lost Tazia, the woman I was going to marry. She couldn't handle knowing the next time I left, could be the last time she saw me. After my accident, she broke our engagement and is now with another man, the mother of his children, and living on the other side of the world."

I opened my mouth to respond, but he lifted his hand and continued, "Ashur is a good man, but he deserves better from you. Just as Tazia deserved better from me. If you can't leave Solon, there are other options."

"It's not that easy. I can't be part of Solon and first lady."

"Yes, it is, but you refuse to see it."

My fingers closed around the levered handle of the metal door, and I closed my eyes. Could I do both roles?

I shook the thought from my head.

Kartik saw my reaction and shook his head. "Stubborn."

Pushing open the door, I entered into the kitchen of

the house and was bombarded with the scent of simmering food and spices.

It always felt so comfortable here. Kartik had turned this place into a home. A home for all the agents who constantly passed through, with a hot meal and a comfortable bed available at all times. He'd lost the only woman he would ever think of marrying and the consolation was a hodgepodge of men and women from all over the world he cared for as his family.

I'd heard the longing in his voice when he'd mentioned Tazia, and it felt like as if his words were a foreshadowing of my future.

A life without Ashur made my stomach hurt and a wave of nausea bubble up.

"Kar?" I said.

"Yes."

"I guess it's too late to go back home?" I knew the answer but asked anyway.

"Yes."

"Then I'll do as you suggested. I'll coordinate from the trucks."

"I'm glad you came to your senses. I'll relay the change to the team. You have exactly eighteen minutes to get changed and grab a bite to eat before we make the drive to the monitoring point."

CHAPTER SEVENTEEN

I wiped my forehead for the tenth time in less than an hour as I scanned the cliffs near the compound where Ameera was held. The informant we had inside the stronghold had confirmed Ameera's presence about an hour earlier, and he knew that there was a plan to move her. This made it even more urgent to get her out.

My decoy had been spotted on the road to Karachi and would arrive in time for the scheduled meeting.

I climbed down from the roof of the military surveillance truck I was using to command the mission and entered the cab. This technically wasn't a truck, it was what I would call the result of a wild threesome between a hummer, a van, and a tank. It was armored in a way to keep the cab safe from gunfire with a painted exterior that camouflaged into the dusty, desert like, mountainous landscape of the area. The interior had two compartments, one for the driver and a separate space that housed ammo, surveillance monitors, and two small chairs.

I slid into a seat that gave me a view of the screens monitoring each of our team members and the windows outside the vehicle.

"Commander, here you go."

I took my canteen from Kade, the operations lead. Kade was a thirty-something former marine who preferred the life of Solon agent to a life behind the desk of his family's Fortune 500 company. His sandy-blond hair was cut military short, and his physique was that of a man who spent hours in the gym, all ripped muscles and bulk.

I liked to think of him as the Hulk without the green coloring.

Lifting the bottle to my lips, I gulped down a large quantity of water, hoping the cool liquid would settle my stomach. I'd felt this uneasiness from the moment we'd gotten into the desert trucks, and it had gotten more intense over the last half hour.

"Do you get the feeling this isn't going to go according to plan?"

"Yes, ma'am. Something seems off. I've informed the lookout to keep a vigilant eye for anything unusual. I have two posted outside the truck and there are four positioned at various points within a half-mile perimeter."

I was glad I wasn't the only one restless. But that only added to my worry. If this went wrong, I wasn't sure how I was going to explain it to Ashur or even Tyler. I almost cringed thinking about how pissed Tyler was going to be once he learned I'd deliberately kept him in the dark about my plans.

Yep, I sucked at letting go of the reins.

"Contact the on-ground team lead. See what's going on."

He nodded, pulling out a satellite phone.

As he talked, I noticed on the screen vehicles a few miles away coming in our direction from one of the roads leading out of the cliffs.

Oh fuck. No one was supposed to be on this road. All the hairs on the back of my neck stood up.

"Kade. We've got unidentified vehicles approaching."

He pulled the phone from his ear. "We've got another problem."

"What?"

"The team just penetrated the compound and Ameera isn't there."

"What?" My gaze went to the fleet coming down the dirt road along the cliffs. "Fuck, that has to be her in the Hummer. I need a closer look."

I shifted to a computer connected to a positioning satellite and began keying codes that would give me detailed images of the area.

As the visuals came through, it was clear the group

coming toward us was protecting a Hummer in the center of their convoy of large supply trucks.

There was no doubt Ameera was being moved.

Immediately, I sent warnings to the team and Kartik. He'd have copters in the air within minutes. He may no longer be an active part of the organization, but it wouldn't stop him from joining in when a mission was in his backyard.

Once I received the green light that we would have support within a few minutes, I released the breath I hadn't known I was holding.

"Commander, we have to get you out of here."

"What? Hell no. Ameera's in there. If the team doesn't get here, we have to stop them."

"There are only six of us here. There's no way to handle the situation."

"Are you kidding me? We've handled bigger situations than this."

"Yes." He sighed. "But circumstances are different. Your value as a hostage is a hundred times greater than Ameera's."

"This isn't your call." I grabbed the rifle from the storage case. I would snipe every one of the motherfuckers before they got past us with Ameera. I will not let the sister of my heart live another day as a prisoner.

"But it's mine." Tyler's very pissed-off voice came over the communications speaker.

"Not on your life." I gathered my pack and slung it over my shoulder as I moved to climb on top of the truck. "Shouldn't you be at an important meeting or something? I'm busy right now, Tyler. Get lost."

"I would be at a meeting, but my hard-headed director decided to play vigilante and leave the country without telling anyone. I had to find out from the board. Are you fucking crazy?"

"I don't have time for this. I have a convoy coming toward us and a mission to lead."

"Negative, ghost rider. Your ass should be on American soil instead of in Asia. I'd order you home if I thought there was any chance you'd listen."

"I don't take orders from you, so can it. I outrank you."

"Not for this one."

"You don't."

"I do."

My heart stopped. The only way he'd have rank on me was if the board assigned him the lead.

"Dammit, Tyler. I will get her back."

"Not at the cost of your life. The report says there are five armed trucks. Even if you went G.I. Jane, you wouldn't be able to win."

"I can snipe each of them before they know what happened. If you remember, I'm a ten times better shot than you." As I turned, Kade blocked my way to the door, crossing his tree-trunk arms.

"Sorry, Commander." I tried to shove him, but he barely budged. "I have orders. Including the use of force to keep you safe."

"Tyler, tell Kade to move or I won't hesitate to shoot him."

"Not going to happen. You aren't thinking straight, and that is a surefire way to endanger Ameera's life. Do you think they'll hand her over without a fight? They'd put a bullet in her head before we even get within yards of her. What would you do if it were any other agent in your situation?"

The fight left my body. I wasn't calm enough to handle this. I was too close to the situation. I'd pull anyone else from the assignment if they had a personal connection to the target.

"What am I supposed to do here, Tyler?" I kept the quiver from my voice, but barely. "She's within reach."

"Exactly what you told me when she went missing. You said I had to think logically. Any wrong move could mean her life."

I had used those words to keep Tyler from resigning from his role in Ashur's admiration. Now I heard the same words.

Think, Tara. This isn't only about Ameera. It is about Ashur and you too.

"I hate it when you're right. I'll wait for backup."

"No, Tara. You are not part of this at all."

"Dammit, Tyler. I will not sit by and let the men save the fucking day."

"This has nothing to do with men and women. Hell, the team is half female. This has to do with the fact you are the first lady and you have a duty to our country, whether you like it or not."

"I hate you so much right now." I let my shoulders sag.

I'd wait until the team arrived and then make the call whether I was part of the operation or not.

"Don't even think about it, Tara."

"What?"

"I know you. We were partners for years on different assignments. Kade has orders to tie you down if you even think of stepping off the truck."

I glared at the smirk on Kade's face. "I'll do it, Commander."

There was no way that I could take him, even on my most fit of days. The guy was built like a tank and probably outweighed me by a hundred and fifty pounds.

"Stop calling me that," I gritted out, threw my rifle on the floor, and sat down on the chair near a bank of monitors, folding like a pissed-off toddler. Yes, it was childish but fuck, I was useless.

He laughed. "You're kind of cute when you're annoyed."

"Kade, I should warn you, she will find her revenge. Be

prepared for an assignment following some pretty playboy through the Thai underground."

The change in Kade's face had me almost losing my irritation at being useless. I'd never put a beast of a man in a situation where he wouldn't have any hope of blending in.

My phone buzzed, and I glanced down. It was a text from Ashur. Of all the times to hear from him, it was now.

Hello, First Lady, heard you aren't well. I'll call later tonight to check on you.

I texted back.

I'm okay, just feeling a bit trapped and irritable.

A second later his response came.

If it's any consolation, I'd rather be in bed next to you making sure you're getting rest, rather than here. Miss you.

A huge wave of guilt hit me. I'd lied to leave and now I'd lied to Ashur. I was digging a bigger and bigger hole for myself.

"Ty, how's Ashur doing?"

"As well as can be expected when dealing with countries who are still upset by his predecessor's decisions."

I knew any trade agreements would be long fought. The tariffs President Edgar had enacted had caused a major economic ripple effect throughout the world, including manufacturers and farmers in the US who conducted business with international companies. It had been a huge cluster of unhappiness that resulted in mass layoffs around the world and the closing of many businesses. Hopefully the Oslo Summit would have some compromises and restore relationships with trade partners.

I didn't envy Ashur the task he had.

All of a sudden, the whole truck jerked, and my chair slammed into the side wall. I staggered to stand and checked for Kade. He was already outside.

"Ty. Can you hear me?"

There was no response—the communications satellite was probably damaged.

The sound of gunfire echoed all around me. I grabbed my pistols, tucked them into the front and back of my pants and under my shirt and then inserted my communications earpiece. I hoped Kade had had enough time to put his in. As I checked to make sure my guns were concealed, I paused. I could swear I heard Ameera's voice.

My heartbeat accelerated at a deafening pace.

My girl was here. I pushed open the door.

A second before I jumped, I screamed into the empty truck, "Ty. If you're hearing this, Ameera's here. Get word to Kartik and the team that we're under fire."

After a quick prayer, I dropped to the ground. I searched the area, trying my hardest to see and breathe through the haze of dust in the air. I pulled a scarf from the back pocket of my mission pants and wrapped it around my nose and mouth.

I maneuvered around the side of the surveillance vehicle and noticed a truck similar to the supply trucks within the convoy had crashed into us. How the hell could they have gotten here so fast? We still had a good twenty minutes before they could maneuver the cliffs to reach us.

As I moved forward, I noticed bodies everywhere. Thank God none of them were my team, but they weren't Awan's, either. The uniforms were too formal and noticeable. Awan's men went out of their way to remain inconspicuous.

I scanned the area for other trucks but only found a high-end luxury Hummer. This could only belong to someone who had money and status and needed others to know it.

Hamir Ustaf.

Dear God, the convoy had been a decoy. How the hell had the satellites not picked this up? Then it hit me. They'd come through the underground tunnels near the base of the mountain. According to reports, an earthquake had caused the tunnels to cave in, but it looked like in the past few years Awan had rebuilt them.

Fuck, fuck, fuck. Hamir must have found out I was meeting with Awan. The only reason he'd be here was to pick up Ameera.

"Kade," I whispered into my wrist mic, "do you copy?"

A faint static came through my earpiece.

"Copy. You need to return to the truck. There are men

circling the area. We've taken down twelve, but there are two at large."

"Do you have a visual on Ameera?"

"Negative. I repeat, return to the safety of the truck."

"Not going to happen."

"I insist."

"Your insistence is noted."

A growl of frustration came over my earpiece. "From my spot I have a visual on you but there are a few blind spots. Be careful."

I smiled—I was probably frustrating the hell out of Kade. He was such a by-the-book kind of guy—like Ashur. It was probably the military aspect of their training.

Thoughts of Ashur began to bombard me. We'd moved to such a nice place in our relationship, but I'd built it all on a lie. How was I going to explain this?

I pushed the worry aside. I had more important things to think about, like putting a bullet in Hamir Ustaf's head and ridding his daughter and the world of his presence.

Just as I moved to the side of the truck that had collided with ours, I heard footsteps.

I whirled and quickly crouched down and slowly moved backward toward my truck.

"We know you are there, First Lady. Come out now, or your precious friend is guaranteed to die," a man said in heavily accented English.

I saw the shadow of two sets of feet.

"Don't listen to them, T. My bastard brother thinks he can auction you to Ashur. The first chance you get, put a fucking bullet—" The words were muffled by a cry and then a grunt as one of the shadows fell to the ground.

Anger roared in my ears. I would kill the motherfucker if it was the last thing I did. Tarik Ustaf would have a target on his head until the job was done. I'd make sure of it. Hopefully I'd get father and son at the same time. Nothing like getting two rotten birds with one stone.

"Stay right there, First Lady." The Urdu words were accompanied by a barrel of a gun pressed into the back of my head.

Oh God. I was so angry that I hadn't noticed someone coming from behind me. I knew better than to let my temper get the best of me. I was losing my edge.

I lifted my arms and turned slowly, making sure to move in a way not to reveal I had guns tucked into my waistband.

I stared at Hamir Ustaf, the man who'd caused this mess. He wore a scarf covering his face, but those eyes gave him away: crystal blue, the exact shade of Ameera's. He was dressed in combat gear that was too over the top and shiny to be anything but for show.

This man had serious small dick syndrome.

"What kind of piece of shit father allows his daughter to be beaten?"

"The kind that prefers women to know their place. She could have killed Tarik in the crash. She needs discipline."

"Too bad it was my truck and not you she hit." I spit in his face. "You're filth in shiny clothing."

Hamir lifted his hand to slap me but stopped the instant he heard his son's voice.

"No, Abbu. You can't hurt her. The world will turn against us if they see any marks on her body. Remember she is a means to an end."

Tarik came into sight with Ameera.

Oh God, what had they done to her? Her signature locks were cropped so close that it looked as if someone had taken a razor to her head. Ameera cradled the side of her face, where I assumed Tarik had punched her, and blood seeped from wounds on the side of her mouth and her left ear.

I clenched my fists.

She'd lost a lot of weight but didn't look malnourished. As I examined her closer, I noticed her injuries were fresh, more than likely sustained in the last twenty-four hours. This would be a constant in her life if Hamir had had a chance to get her out.

"Where are your men?"

Hamir brought my attention back to him, but before I turned my gaze to him, I saw Ameera tap her stomach.

Sneaky girl. She knew I was armed. It was something we'd learned to do when we were in field training. If I could get close enough we could take these assholes down.

"I could ask you the same question."

"Don't play games. You've cost me too much. You have exactly one minute to tell me."

"Or what?"

He turned his gun to Ameera. *"I will shoot her. You risked your life and your husband's career for her. I'm sure you'd do anything to protect her."*

"Shoot me, you asshole." Ameera shouted in Urdu as she thrashed in Tarik's arms and tried to kick out toward Hamir. *"I'd rather die than let you sell me to that old man whose money you need so much. You aren't my father. Travis Angelo is my father. You're nothing but a sperm donor."*

As soon as the words were out, Tarik slapped Ameera again and then threw her against the side of the truck. I jumped in her direction, catching her before she slammed onto the ground. I cradled her body against mine as we slid to the dirt.

"You need to show him some respect. He is your king. You will never speak to him like that again."

"She is an American citizen, asshole. She has no king."

The sounds of helicopters echoed off the mountains, and I knew our support would be here any moment.

"Abbu, we have to get out of here. The military is doing a sweep."

"Get them into the car."

Ameera's fingers worked their way under my shirt, and I felt her pull the piece in the front of my pants out.

I rocked Ameera as if to comfort her and tugged out the gun at the back of my waist.

"Let's go." Tarik grabbed my arm, hurling me up.

I twisted out of his hold and held up my gun. "I'm not going anywhere with you."

"Very brave, but you have only one gun and there are two of us."

"Wrong." Ameera stood and without another word, shot Hamir in the head.

"No." Tarik charged Ameera.

I lifted the cocked gun, but before I could fire, a bullet pierced his forehead, and he dropped to the ground.

In the next moments, two helicopters landed, Solon agents grabbed both Ameera and me, and we immediately lifted off.

CHAPTER EIGHTEEN

A week after returning from Pakistan, I sat in the same room where I'd dressed for my wedding and prepared to have my first official dinner as the first lady. I was feeling jittery and restless. Like I needed to do something with my energy.

Maybe my anxiety had to do with the fact that I kept waiting for the shoe to drop from Hamir's death.

International outlets had reported a rebel group loyal to the Burki, the original ruling clan of Janestan, as the ones responsible for Hamir's and Tarik's deaths. It helped that the Burki family had claimed they'd received word of an assassination plan to slaughter any and all dependents of their clan gave weight to the necessity of removing Hamir from power.

Thankfully, Kartik had used his connections to erase any and all evidence of our involvement. He'd gone as far as staging Hamir's and Tarik's bodies near the Janestan boarder to keep nosey reporters away from the area where everything went down.

This should have eased my mind, but all I kept thinking was that it seemed too neat and tidy for a mission of this caliber.

Then there was the fact that I'd had no contact with Ameera after we landed on Kartik's estate. Solon had essentially whisked her away to an undisclosed location. I knew it was standard procedure after a hostage situation, but all I wanted was to have a few words with her and give her a big hug. She was my sister in everything but blood and I couldn't reach her.

I released a deep breath, shifted in my seat, and rubbed my back.

Damn, my body still ached from the rescue. Fieldwork was no longer my favorite thing.

Normally, it would only take me a few days of locking myself in my house to recover. But this time, my body was screaming for sleep and sex. The need for sleep was normal but the desire for sex was a new one. And the fact, Ashur had spent the last ten days in Oslo and then traveled to various countries in Europe hadn't helped.

I had needs, and the man wasn't here to satisfy them.

Ameera had told me that sex quenched the adrenaline and endorphins released from high-stress situations.

Thank God Ashur's plane had landed a half hour ago.

The moment we were alone tonight, I planned to jump his ass and not come up for air until I was satisfied.

"Drink. This will settle your stomach." Walter, my makeup artist, finished applying my lipstick and then set a sparkling water bottle with a straw in front of me.

"Thanks." I picked up the water and drank deep. "How'd you know?"

"I have my ways. Plus, I can tell when a woman is restless. And that my dear, you are."

"Since when did you become the expert on women?"

"Since forever. I have five sisters. I'm the last-ditch effort to get a boy and I'm the father of two girls."

I smiled at the mention of Walter's twins. He and his partner of fifteen years had wanted to adopt for over a decade, with no success. Then they were given the opportunity to have biological children of their own via a surrogate. They jumped at the chance and now he was the proud daddy of two four-year-olds who adored him.

"How are Allison and Trinity?"

"Nice try." Walter closed the lid to his makeup case and came toward me with a compact and brush. "No trying to change the subject. What gives? Man trouble already?"

If he only knew. Well, that wasn't true. I'd have to be around Ashur to have trouble with him.

When the fuck had I become so needy?

I lifted my hand to pinch the bridge of my nose.

"I swear if you touch your face, I will smack your hand and I don't care if you are the first lady."

I scowled at Walter, who was putting away makeup pallets in his roller case and had his back to me.

"How can you see what I'm doing from over there?"

"It's a bad habit you've always had. Why do you think I threaten you with bodily harm if you mess with the perfection I created?"

"Conceited much?" I muttered.

"It's not conceited if it's a fact. Now what gives? From the news reports, you've been locked away in your ivory tower sick from a severe cold."

I winced inside and then glance at Casey, who was standing in the corner trying not to smirk at my irritation. He'd insisted it was best to leak I was sick to the press so they wouldn't snoop, because no one wanted to see a runny-nosed first lady. And I guessed he was right, since all requests for interviews and meetings had stopped for the last week.

"Stop stalling and tell me what the issue is so Walter can help solve your woes."

"I doubt you can fix my issue. I'm just..."

Walter finished my sentence. "Horny?"

My cheeks reddened. "Umm."

"So, I take it the 'hot president' is a rock star in bed."

"I'm not answering that."

"You're such a prude sometimes. But I'm glad he thaws

your ice-queen, all-business demeanor. It's nice to know there's a man that can get you all hot and bothered, even if he is a politician."

"Thanks, I think."

"Don't scowl, you'll ruin all my work. It was a compliment. Although I've never envisioned you being a girl who's content doing charity projects while her politician husband is off saving the world."

That was something I was going to have to get used to too, but after Ameera's rescue, it was what I'd set as my future.

I couldn't live the uncertainty of the high-stress life anymore, especially if Ashur and I were going to have a baby. I wanted to give our child the life my parents had given me—safe, secure, and full of love despite the craziness of the outside world.

"Who says I can't save the world with my projects? If you remember, No Bride was something I started."

"I see your point. Then why are you so restless?"

"Because, as you said. She's horny," Ashur's deep raspy voice answered from behind us.

I turned my head in Ashur's direction and nearly swallowed my tongue. He was dressed to the nines in a tux similar to the one he'd worn to our wedding day. He looked debonair with an edge of danger.

His eyes burned with desire adding fuel to the inferno of need pulsing deep in my pussy.

"Let's go, Mrs. Kumar. We are due in the reception room in ten minutes." He walked toward me with a wicked grin. Then, as I stood, he whispered in my ear, "And if you're a good girl, I promise to fuck you senseless and make up for neglecting you these past ten days."

I RELEASED A SIGH OF RELIEF AS I SAT DOWN ON MY favorite bench in the rose garden and kicked off my heels.

The reception and dinner had gone off without a hitch and now the dancing was in full swing. All in all, my worry about not knowing what I was doing was more my uneasiness with my role than the actual duties themselves. If I could learn the ropes and become a top-notch Solon agent, then I could suck it up and do my best as the first lady.

"Can I join you, Tara?"

I smiled and turned to the Viking who approached me. Xander Alexi was what some would call a cross between a Norwegian and Greek god. He had the striking blond hair and crystal blue eyes from his mother's Nordic genetics and the tanned golden hue and long lean build of his father's Mediterranean side. I remembered when Sam had first introduced me to him, I'd thought he was a pretty face with little in the brains department, when in fact he was a member of Mensa and probably one of the smartest people on campus.

We'd had an attraction from the start, nothing like what happened with Ashur but one that was filled with fun, friendship, and mutual enjoyment. Our affair hadn't gone beyond our years at Harvard, but our friendship had developed into something more like a brother-sister relationship. Enough so that I'd introduced him to the woman who'd become his wife and the love of his life.

"Xander. How are you?" I gave him a quick hug. "Where's Carina?"

"Over there." He gestured over his shoulder to the windows.

In the distance a beautiful brunette danced with Xander's father. She was a little over six months pregnant, wearing four-inch heels with her gown and smiling without a care in the world.

"Those are serious pregnancy goals."

"My love would kill someone if they tried to take her designer shoes from her. I have a feeling she'll be in labor and walking to the car in her favorite Louboutin sandals."

"Come sit." I tapped the bench. "Take a load off."

He joined me and we stared into the night.

"You might as well tell me what's on your mind," I said. "I can tell you're dying to say something."

"I'm sorry I couldn't be at the wedding."

"Honestly I'm glad you didn't brave the chaos. Ash and

I considered running away at least twenty times."

"That would have made some amazing headlines."

I couldn't help but laugh. "Thankfully, neither of us were brave enough to actually go through with it."

"Do you regret not letting the world you two were already married?"

My smile dropped. "Who told you?"

"I have my sources." Xander kept his gaze straight. "Ashur did exactly what I would have done if I lost Carina and had an opportunity to get her back. What I want to know is why you would marry him? And don't say money, because that's bullshit. If you truly needed money, all you'd have to was ask Samina or me. We'd have happily handed over a chunk of our inheritances."

"You know why."

I could never hide anything from Xander. This was why we made better friends and lovers. He called me on my bullshit.

"Does he know?"

"No."

"Going to tell him?"

I stayed quiet. How could I tell Ashur I wanted to tear up the contract when he may not want me at all once he learned what I'd done or who I was.

"I'm going to take your silence as a 'I'm thinking about it'."

"You're such an ass."

"Takes one to know one. Now I have another question for you."

I glanced at him. He was giving me his serious vibe all of a sudden.

"Want to tell me how Ameera is doing after your adventure in Pakistan?"

I glanced around to make sure no one heard him. If Xander knew about the operation, he was involved in things more than his shipping empire.

"Who the fuck do you work for, Xan?"

"It doesn't matter. All you need to know is that we're on the same side."

I knew it. I should have picked up on it years ago. Xander moved too fluidly for an international playboy. Even when he seemed relaxed, he would scan his surroundings. I'd chalked it up to an eccentricity of being known throughout the world and wanting to keep an eye out for paparazzi.

"MI6?" I asked knowing he would never admit it.

He smirked and then countered, "Solon?"

"So that explains why we get along so well. We both have secrets neither of our significant others can know about."

"Carina knows. I told her as soon as I knew she was the one."

"Really?"

"Yes. She deserved to know and make the decision if

she could live with the life I led. Ashur deserves the same. His future could depend on it."

Guilt hit me. All I'd done was keep secrets from Ashur. Even when he tried and tried to get me to open up, I kept quiet. Now on top of everything, I'd gotten involved in an incident that could destroy his career.

"How do I tell him?"

"That's something I can't help you with. All I can say is do it sooner rather than later." He picked up my hand and kissed my fingers. "Hamir's sons have started a full-scale search for anyone with information on how their father and brother died. They know as well as we do that the Barki don't have the means or capacity to launch an attack on their father or his convoy. This is about to blow up. Make sure Ashur is prepared."

I released a deep breath. I had no choice. I couldn't let Ashur find out from someone else.

"I'll do it tonight."

A throat cleared behind us, making me stiffen.

"Mrs. Kumar," Casey said. "The president is looking for you."

I turned in the direction of the ballroom windows and winced. Ashur had a death glare focused in our direction.

This was fabulous—not only would I have to explain my sordid past, but now I'd have to explain why I was sitting in a garden with my ex.

There went any hopes of a night of hot, raunchy sex.

CHAPTER NINETEEN

I walked into the study of the master suite a little before midnight to find Ashur sitting on the loveseat by the window. He stared at me, sipping his scotch. He'd thrown his tuxedo jacket over the arm of a nearby chair and his bowtie was undone. He had a brooding, almost predatory gleam in his gaze that had my heartbeat accelerating.

"You left your own party."

"And."

I hesitated, not knowing what to do. He was in a mood and I wasn't sure if I should try to placate the beast rumbling under the surface or run out of the room.

I wasn't one to run, so that left dealing with my surly husband.

"It looks bad if the president decides he's tired and disappears."

"I had enough of political jockeying. Now I have four words for you."

"And they are?"

"Take off your clothes."

"What?"

The last thing I expected was for him to touch me. The anger radiating off him when Xander and I had returned to the ballroom could have killed a battalion. It was as if the whole room had gotten cold, and the fact that he'd all but ignored me for the rest of the night hadn't gone unnoticed by the guests.

My husband had gone from hot and couldn't stop touching me to wanting nothing to do with me. Now we were back to...well, I wasn't sure what this was.

"Take off your clothes, Tara."

The roughness of his words sent a shiver straight to my pussy, making me forget the uncertainty of a second earlier.

"The contract says for my money, I get two children. That means I get to fuck you until our goal is achieved."

I swallowed. "Ashur, is this about Xander? We were only talking."

"Why would it be about the man who replaced me? Why would it be about the man who had you longer than I did? Why would it be about a man you still love?"

"He is nothing more than a brother. He is married to

the woman he loves more than life. Hell, I was one of his grooms' people."

A growl erupted from his lips as he stood and stalked toward me. "That so-called brother of yours has seen you naked. He's seen you come. He's seen what is mine. He was kissing your hand tonight as a lover would."

"Oh, for the love of God, Ashur. Were you a monk while we were apart?" I cocked a hand on my hip, lifting my chin and trying desperately to keep my heart from exploding out of my chest. "From everything I learned, you fucked every eligible heiress around, not to mention all the military bunnies who put out for a man in uniform."

"So, you kept tabs on me."

"The same can be said for you." I glowered up at him.

Dammit, why the fuck was he so tall? I probably looked like a toddler trying to intimidate a giant.

"You were mine from the time I popped your cherry. The fact we lived separate lives for over a decade doesn't change that. Besides, I wanted to know about every man who's touched your body."

"And what conclusion did you come to? Tell me, how many men have I been with?"

"More than I like but less than what the public likes to believe."

When I'd made my first headline, rumors had swirled I was mistress to a Middle Eastern prince, then over the years I'd been linked to various influential personalities around the world. My relationships with each of the men were completely platonic but I hadn't corrected the misconception, since it allowed me access to social circles I otherwise wouldn't have been privy to interact with.

Outside of Ashur and Xander, I'd had one other relationship. And I wouldn't have called it a true relationship. It was more a casual way to scratch an itch with another Solon agent, whenever we'd been in the same place at the same time. The last time we'd seen each other was five years ago, right before I'd taken on the director role, where we'd decided it was better for him not to have a fling with his boss. He was now married and the father of two and one of Solon's best agents.

"What makes you so sure I haven't slept with all those men?"

"Because I know you. There has to be more between you and your lovers than mutual attraction. At the least, there would have to be friendship."

"What do we have, Ashur?"

He gripped my waist and then ran his palm up my ribcage, thumbing my nipple through my dress. "What's between us puts everything either of us had before to shame. We are as complicated as it gets, full of entanglements, need, and a binding history. There's a word for it, but you're too scared to admit it."

I kept quiet. Admitting he was right would only cause more pain for us in the end.

"Now, Tara. Take off your clothes so I can fuck you so hard that with every step you take tomorrow you'll feel the twinge of how I imprinted myself onto your body."

Without thought, I reached behind me to open my dress. But before I could grasp the zipper, Ashur's hand caught mine, taking control and lowering it himself.

I took in a deep breath as the corseted dress gave way, allowing my lungs to expand to their fullest capacity.

"Step out."

I followed his command and then reached down to take off my shoes, when he said, "Leave on the heels. I want to fuck you with the red stilettos on."

Goosebumps prickled my skin.

"Now the rest."

I nodded, unclasping my bra, letting it fall to the ground, and then shimmying out of my underwear.

"Brace your hands on the bed."

Setting my palms flat on the duvet, I focused on the decorative pillows sitting along the headboard. Butterflies fluttered deep in the pit of my stomach, and a low throbbing of arousal grew stronger with each second.

The sound of a drawer opening and shutting reached my ears and then a tube of lubricant was dropped near the fingers of my right hand.

Goosebumps prickled my skin and my breathing became a bit shallow.

I knew what this meant. He was the only one who'd

ever fucked me there. I'd confessed this to him during our honeymoon. And now he was ready to assert his claim on me, to remind me I'd only ever allowed him the pleasure.

"Since you became my wife, I've taken your cunt, your mouth, your breast, but I have yet to take you here." His fingers glided along the cleft of my ass cheeks. "Tonight, I want it all."

He pressed against my back, telling me without words to lower my head to the bed. Following his unspoken directive, I rested my forehead against my folded arms and positioned my ass into the air. My legs instinctively separated to keep my balance. Thank goodness for the height my heels gave me, or this wouldn't have been a comfortable position to maintain.

Why was I so okay with this...this bossiness...this hunger he had to claim me?

Because you want to be his.

When we were younger, this was all about learning each other's bodies, about giving each other something neither of us had experienced. We'd bumbled through the awkwardness and found pleasure after experimenting for a time.

Tonight was completely different. Ashur knew exactly what to do and I...well, I may not have had the experiences I could only assume Ashur had but I knew what to expect. The discomfort, the fullness, and the pleasure.

I jumped a fraction as a warm hand grabbed my ankle

and hot breath skimmed up the length of my calf. Ashur kissed, licked, and nipped at my skin, paying extra attention the area behind my knee. The fingers of his free hand followed the same path as his mouth on my other leg.

The sensation sent shivers down my spine and straight to my clit and nipples. A rush of air left my lungs. This slow perusal of my body was not something I expected from him, especially with the volatility that had been radiating from him when I entered the room.

This man confused the hell out of me.

When Ashur's exploration led to the lower curve of my bottom, he bit one cheek. I yelped but found myself liking the sting. Heat bloomed deep inside me, causing my folds to grow damp and swollen.

His finger pulled my cheeks apart, exposing my slick pussy and the tight rosette of my ass. His tongued all the way from my clitoral nub to hole he would claim tonight, moving back and forth, creating a heady mix of sensation I could only describe as forbidden ecstasy.

My legs began to shake as an orgasm crept its way into my throbbing pussy. I bit my lip as a moan escaped, and threw my head back, waiting for the pleasure to course through me. Except it didn't come.

I released a frustrated breath, lifting my head to glare at him over my shoulder. He locked his amber eyes with mine as his lips tugged up at the corners.

"Is there something you want?"

"I need to come."

"Soon." His focus moved back to my pussy, and before I knew it, his tongue was piercing my sopping folds and deep into my core.

My legs gave out. However, I was held in the same position by Ashur's strong hold on my thighs. His grip was tight, owning, telling me I'd have bruises in the shapes of his fingers on each thigh. He spread my legs wide and pushed my knees onto the bed, all the while eating my pussy as a man starved.

The rhythm he created made my mind cloud, releasing an addictive sense of euphoria. By the time I registered the distinct click of a tube opening, Ashur was pressing a lubed finger into the tight hole of my ass. My first instinct was to clench tight, to pull away.

"Relax, baby. I'll make it good for you, but I have to prepare you."

I nodded and released a deep breath, allowing my muscles to loosen. A slow burn pierced my opening as he worked his way in, inch by inch. The sensation shouldn't feel so good, but it did. When a second finger joined the first, the pleasure-pain was too much and my empty pussy began to contract. I arched my back, unable to control the spasms talking over.

A sharp bite to my ass brought me out of my orgasm.

"I say when you come, and you will not come until my cock is deep inside your ass."

"I hate you so much right now."

"No you don't, love. You're just frustrated that I'm not giving you what you want."

"Ashu, please," I whined, but he ignored me.

He held me on the cusp of orgasm, working my snug passage with his fingers and my swollen aching pussy with the thumb of his other hand.

Tears streamed down my face. My body screamed for release and just when I thought I'd tell him to fuck off and take care of my desire myself, cool liquid slid along the valley of my ass cheeks.

My focus immediately snapped to Ashur as the hum of need continued to throb deep in my core.

"Ashu," I whispered.

My arousal cooled as it wept down the insides of my thighs, mixing with the liquid smoothness of the lubricant.

"Shhh." His lips grazed the lower dip of my back.

In the next second, the naked hot heat of Ashur's body molded against my back, making me moan.

His lube-covered cock slid against my clit, sending shockwaves through my body that had me nearly collapsing. Ashur's hand snaked around my abdomen, holding me close to him.

He glided his erection up my slit to the swollen, soaked passage to my pussy, pushing in for a brief second before he moved to the puckered entrance of my ass.

"Now, I take what is mine. What has always been

mine." He gripped my hip as the head of his cock pressed through the tight ring of muscles.

I released a deep breath and tried not to tighten up, knowing it would only cause me discomfort. Sweat dampened my skin as his velvety cock pushed all the way in.

I cried out. It was almost too much, the fullness, the burning, the need. My nails dug into his forearms and my back arched.

He immediately held still, giving me time to adjust.

"Christ, you're so tight," Ashur said through clenched teeth. "Fuck. Tara. I have to move."

He pulled out all the way and surged back in. Tingles and goosebumps broke out all over my skin and the low hum of my unquenched release ignited into a full inferno.

His fingers moved from my hip over my pelvis to the bundle of nerves at the apex of my pussy. He strummed my clit, matching the pace to that of his pummeling cock.

"Oh God, Ashu. Oh, God. Why does this feel so good?"

"Because it's us. This has only ever belonged to us."

I couldn't help myself, I tilted my head back to look into his eyes and see if he meant what I thought I'd heard.

"It's true baby. You're the only woman I've ever fucked like this."

"Why?" I asked between the force of his thrusts.

"Because it's intimate on the highest level. It requires trust, not just need."

My lips trembled and I whispered, "It's the same for me. Kiss me, Ashu."

He lowered his mouth to mine. Our kiss was filled with an emotion I knew would leave me in shambles when all my secrets came out. I pushed the thoughts back and lost myself in Ashur.

His finger and cock continued their onslaught of passion on my body, and within a few more strokes, my body was detonating.

I pulled free of our kiss, bucking and arching as my orgasm washed over me. Everything inside me clenched and a guttural cry echoed in my ear as Ashur's pistoning cock grew harder. In the next second he came, pushing all his weight onto my back and releasing with an intensity I'd never experienced with him before.

ABOUT TWENTY MINUTES AFTER THE MOST EARTH-shattering orgasm of my life, Ashur picked me up, carried me to the top of our bed, and laid me down as if I were a precious jewel.

"Let me get cleaned up and then we can go to bed."

I could only nod as he pressed his lips to my forehead and moved toward the bathroom. My body was too lethargic to muster the strength to budge a muscle. A few minutes later, I felt the heat of a warm washcloth glide between my legs. I moaned, enjoying the gentle caress of the damp cloth. When Ashur finished caring for me, he crawled onto the bed, pulling my body against his.

He held me for what felt like hours. I listened to the steady beat of his heart.

"It's okay, love."

I remained quiet. This was far from okay. What we'd just shared had changed the level of our relationship.

Our raw, need-filled coupling was more than sex, more than him marking his territory. I'd just handed everything I was over to him. The urge to weep and run warred with wanting never to let this man go.

I'd lost the battle. I couldn't deny it anymore. I couldn't pretend I wasn't in love with him.

Now all I could do was wait and see if he truly felt the same for me or if he loved the illusion of me, the memory of the girl I'd been.

He tilted up my face and kissed me. A kiss so slow and long, one filled with everything I'd ever wanted from him.

He pulled back and murmured against my lips. "I love..."

Before he went further, I covered his mouth with mine. I refused to let him speak words he may regret saying later.

He broke our kiss and stared at me with a tinge of frustration. "Why won't you let me tell you?"

"Ashu, please. I'm not strong enough to hear those words and then have you take them back."

"Do you really think I'd do that to you? Do you really think I'd give you my heart only to steal it away again?"

"You did it before."

"Dammit, Tara. I was twenty-three. Why do you keep holding the past over us?"

"Because I know history will repeat itself."

"What are you hiding? Why are you so afraid to love me and let me love you?"

"Let it go." I sat up, dropping my feet off the side of the bed. "Maybe it's better to stick to our contract. Then we don't have to worry about hurting each other."

"Is that really what you want?"

No, I wanted to scream. *I want the fairytale. I want to have faith that you'll stand by me when you learn the truth of who I am and what I've done.*

"It's for the best." A tear slipped down my cheek as my shoulders slumped.

"Tell me, Tara. Was it only the money that made you agree to marry me?"

I kept quiet and stared at the wall through a wet haze.

I turned to look at him over my shoulder. I opened my lips to respond, but he cut me off.

"Don't. Your initial silence tells me all I wanted to know." His eyes filled with such pain and resignation. "You want to know something?" He ran a hand through his hair.

"I didn't need you to win the election. I never did. I wanted to marry you because you're the only woman I've ever loved. The only woman I will ever love. You were right. You were more a liability than an asset, but I didn't give a damn. You were always it for me. I just wish I was it for you."

Ashur stood from the bed, shrugged on his robe and walked toward the door that connected to the sitting room.

As he yanked the door open, he said over his shoulder, "You want a contract marriage, I'll give you a contract marriage. We'll fuck without emotion, have children, and live separate lives outside the bedroom."

I stood in a numb haze... I'd distorted everything we'd built over the last two years. I destroyed the one thing that meant more to me than anything by keeping my secrets, by refusing to acknowledge how much he meant to me.

He was such a man of pride. Emotions weren't part of his DNA but with me he showed a side no one would believe existed.

God, what had I done?

I slowly dropped onto the bed and curled into a ball and let my stupidity and tears engulf me.

CHAPTER TWENTY

"Oh God, not again." I ran to the toilet and emptied the contents of my stomach.

After the heaving stopped, I rested my body against the surround of the bathtub. I closed my eyes and waited for the next wave of nausea.

This sucked. There was no doubt, I was pregnant.

I hadn't thought anything of it when I missed a period last month since my monthly cycle had been irregular since I was a teen, making it so I could miss a month here and there without worry.

It wasn't until this past week when the constant fatigue and nausea became too much to ignore that I grew suspicious. And then this morning, the vomiting started.

Wasn't a woman supposed to get at least a few hours of respite between bouts of throwing up?

I covered my stomach. "Sorry, kid. I'm happy you're coming, but could you let up for a few minutes?"

My stomach turned again.

"Well, I guess that's my answer. Is this payback for taking you on my mission with me?"

God, I couldn't believe I'd gone to Pakistan pregnant. I could have lost my baby if anything had gone wrong.

"I will never put your life at risk again. Though you did choose a very inconvenient time to make an appearance."

I had to have ovulated during one of the first few times Ashur and I'd had sex. I literally was the bride who got pregnant on her honeymoon.

So, all the fucking Ashur and I had done over the last few weeks was for nothing. He'd kept to his word. We lived separate lives during the day and only met in the bedroom for the sole purpose of producing a child.

I wouldn't lie to myself and say I hadn't enjoyed the sex, Ashur made sure I achieved my orgasm, but it felt so cold. I'd rather have just gone to bed than feel so lonely afterward. We'd become the political couple that made appearances and posed for pictures but barely spent any time together. Gone were the heated discussions and the playful banter. Gone were the hot looks and constant touching.

"I promise, little one. No matter what happens between your daddy and me, you'll never know a day without love. I suck at the wife-and-first-lady thing, but I will rock the mother thing."

The churning in my belly finally stopped, and I pushed up onto my feet. Immediately nausea returned and I grabbed the toilet seat, letting what little was left in my stomach empty.

"I hate you, Jacinta," I muttered to myself and then said to my belly, "Your Samina *Foi* too. I hope your cousins make her gray early."

"Why are you cursing my sister?"

I froze. Ashur had to have heard what I said.

I looked at him. He stared at me with worry and a bit of amusement.

"Go away, Ashur. I don't need you to laugh at my misery." I rested my head on my forearm, praying the nausea would stop.

"Let me help you."

"I think you've done enough. Your super sperm did the job. You won't have to fuck me every night anymore for an heir."

"Do you really think that's the only reason I want you? For God's sake. I've known you were pregnant for over two weeks."

How the fuck could he have known when I only suspected this past week?

"I can see the question so let me answer. I figured it out

when your breasts began to swell and you kept sneaking away for power naps."

"So, my need for sleep gave it away?"

"You are one of those high-energy, sleep-when-I'm-dead women. So, combined with the slight changes in your body, I knew it was either you were coming down with something or as you said, my super sperm did the job."

"Could have given me a clue," I muttered under my breath.

"And just so we're clear, the reason I come to our bed every night is that losing myself in you is the only thing that keeps me going these days."

"Whatever. Go away. Let me vomit in peace." I slid further onto the floor and rested my head on the cool tile.

Was this some sick joke by God? Samina and Jacinta hadn't a day of sickness and here I was, barely a month and a half in and ready to throw in the towel on this pregnancy shit. Maybe I could revise the contract and change it to one child, then I wouldn't have to do this again.

"You hard-headed, stubborn woman. Is it so difficult to depend on me?" Ashur scooped me off the floor, opened the door to the shower, stepped in, and sat me on a long bench in one corner.

"What are you doing?" I batted away Ashur's hands as he tried to pull my dress over my head. "Stop. I don't want a shower."

"You smell like puke."

I opened my mouth to argue, but shut it when I got a whiff of myself.

"Fine, but let me brush my teeth first." I stood and was immediately pushed back down.

"You sit and I'll bring it to you."

Ashur turned on the spray to heat the water before leaving me on the bench to retrieve my toothbrush and toothpaste.

When he returned he was naked and partially aroused.

"Sorry. I can't help it. My cock is always halfway hard whenever you're around."

Without responding, I took the offered brush and scrubbed the pasty vomit aftertaste from my mouth. When I finished, I set the brush on the bench beside me. Steam billowed around us and I leaned my head back against the cool tiled wall, enjoying the sensation of cool and hot.

"Come on, love. Let's get you cleaned up." Ashur gently helped me up. "Let me take care of you and then tuck you into bed."

I sighed and relented.

He washed me from head to toe and then back up again. By the time he was done, the nausea was gone and completely replaced by arousal. Ashur hadn't done anything to purposefully stimulate me, but my body wanted him.

"Ready to come out." His voice was rough and his breath was a bit shallow.

His cock stood straight up, ready for me and making my mouth water.

"Ashu. I..."

"What do you want, Tara?"

"You."

"This isn't why I brought you in here."

I reached for him, wrapping my fingers around his thick, hard, velvety length and pumped my fist up and down.

"I know. I want you, Ashu. I want the need, the passion, not what we've had for the past three weeks. I want it to be more than fucking."

He walked me back, pressing me against the shower wall and trapping the hand enfolded around his cock between us.

"Are you sure? We'd be going outside of the rules of the contract."

"I don't care about that right now. I need you inside me." I tried to rise onto tiptoes in hopes of guiding his cock inside my swollen, aching pussy, but our height difference made it impossible.

He grabbed my thighs and parted them before pressing his cock against my soaked slit.

"This is about us, Tara." His cock pushed in. "Not the contract." He went in a little farther. "Not our child that's inside you. Not the past or the future. Do you understand?"

"Yes," I gasped. "About us right now."

He seated himself to the hilt.

"Being inside you is like heaven." He pulled out and thrust back in. "Don't ever think I want you for anything other than you."

I clenched at his shoulders as my pussy walls contracted around his length.

"Okay." I met each thrust with the rotation of my hips. "Faster, please, I'm almost there."

"Hold on, love. I'll give you what you want."

He adjusted our bodies so he could sit on the bench and positioned my knees so I could ride him. He met each of my movements with the upward motion of his own. It was hard and fast and loud. The sound of our wet bodies pounding against each other echoed off the tile and added to the frantic nature of our need.

He held my gaze as the first of my spasms started and then I flew apart in his arms. The clenching of my swollen pussy muscles pushed Ashur over into his own orgasm and he came deep inside my core.

My phone beeped twenty minutes after Ashur and I crawled into bed. His hand rested against my abdomen, and his breath was slow and steady against my neck.

Another alert sounded, followed by three more

I slowly worked my way out of his arms and reached over to grab my cell.

Meet me in your office. We're about to hit a shit storm. -T

This is an emergency.

Dammit, Tara. Wake the fuck up.

I will come up there to get you.

My stomach dropped, this time not from nausea but a fear that everything was about to come crashing down.

Sliding off the bed, I grabbed my robe, slipping it on and tying it tight around my waist. I exited our room as quietly as possible, so as not to disturb Ashur.

As I made my way to my office, the dread I felt began to weigh on my shoulders. The true test for Ashur was about to come.

I entered my office to find Ameera sitting on a chair in the corner and Tyler pacing.

Ameera immediately jumped up and ran to me, engulfing me in her arms.

"Oh God, Ame. I missed you so much."

Tears streamed down both our faces as we held each other, talking at the same time and probably making sense to no one but the other.

When we finally pulled apart, I studied her beautiful face. She looked almost completely healed with only a few lingering cuts and bruises left, and she'd gained a few pounds. She still had a few more to go before she returned to her curvy bombshell figure but this was a positive sign. Her hair was now a stylish pixie bob, a vast improvement from the almost buzz cut her captors has given her.

"The new look suits you."

"You know how I like to keep things high fashion." She touched the tips of her golden blond hair.

"Now that the reunion is complete, you need to take a look at these. Hamir's sons sent these to the State Department." Tyler handed me his phone.

I scanned through a bunch of images showing someone who looked like me meeting with known terrorists around the world.

"These are doctored. The first time I left the country in two years was only three months ago and these are dated before that."

"The last few aren't."

I scrolled to the last pictures, and my heart sank. Ameera and I held guns and Tarik lay on the ground dead. The barrel of my weapon was aimed at Hamir. The look on my face was complete fury. There was no way anyone could say these pictures were tampered with. The unique design of the diamonds in my wedding band gleamed from the sunlight.

God how could I be so stupid as to forget Hamir loved to record himself driving that damn Hummer. The cameras on the vehicle were the only way they could have gotten the pictures.

There had to be some means of corrupting the original feed.

I pulled out my own cell and began texting the North American tech unit for Solon. After relaying the instructions, I looked up at Tyler. "Tech is going to scrub any data sources associated with Hamir. We have a lock on his servers and satellites."

"It isn't as simple as a few calls to the right people, T," Ameera said and then ran frustrated fingers through her short hair. "This went out to all news media outlets. The Ustafs want revenge and the best way to do it is to ruin your reputation, and in turn, Ashur's."

I closed my eyes, pinching the bridge of my nose. "They're going to paint me as a traitor who negotiates with terrorists."

No one was going to believe the majority of the pictures were fakes. I'd be tried in front of the court of public opinion before an investigation was even launched.

Oh God, Ashur. No one would believe he'd had no knowledge of it.

I should never have agreed to marry him. I knew I was a liability to him, and now it had come true.

"I need to make a few calls to Geneva. They'll have a plan already in the works." I moved over to my desk, settling my hand over my stomach to will the wave of nausea starting to creep up again. As soon as it calmed, I looked between Tyler and Ameera. "The two of you need to completely distance yourself from me and, if at all possible, from each other."

"Pretending Ameera and I don't have a connection, won't be a problem. She's made it very clear that I am her past, not her future." He gave Ame an angry glare and then turned his attention to me. "You, on the other hand, will be impossible. I work for your husband and I am a longtime friend."

"You work for me too. I will not have you tied up in this. That is a direct order."

"Does that mean you aren't stepping down?"

"My job as the director of Solon is the least of my concerns at the moment."

"Only the director outranks me, so unless you're Command, I will ignore any directive coming from you."

"I second what he says." Ameera came to lean over my desk. "If you weren't my ride or die, would you have come to save me? Don't even for a second think I'll let you take the fall for something that's my fault. I will go before the media and claim it was me before I let anything happen to you."

"Dammit. I'm trying to save your careers." I smacked my hand on my desk as tears burned the backs of my eyes. "Because of me, Ashur may be impeached. I won't have your futures on my conscience too."

"If it gives you peace of mind, I will happily step down from my role as a UN ambassador in a heartbeat," Ameera said. "I was planning to transition out of my role there anyway."

"Don't you dare do that. I would never ask you to give up the job you love." I glowered at Ameera, who responded with her own glare.

"And for the record, counselor, that man you refuse to admit you love will survive anything thrown at him. Why do you think his opponents call him an asshole? He doesn't give a shit what anyone says. Plus, he's a fucking tech billionaire."

"He's not an asshole." I dropped my head to the desk. I was the asshole for thinking I could keep who I was from Ashur.

Maybe if I'd told him, this whole mess wouldn't have happened.

"For the love of God, Tara. In all the shit I said, the asshole part is all you got?"

"She heard you. She's just ignoring you."

Tyler came around the desk and crouched in front of me. "T-Rex, time's up. You need to tell Ashur before someone wakes him and gives him the news."

"Someone did wake him," Ashur said from the doorway of my office.

He held up a phone to display the picture of me

holding the gun. Anger, hurt, and betrayal radiated from him.

"When the two of you are finished reporting to your director, I'd like a word with my wife."

I WAITED TEN MINUTES BEFORE SEARCHING OUT Ashur. He needed to calm down and I had to call the board. As I expected, a plan was in the works and would be implemented within the next twenty-four hours.

Being that it was only two o'clock in the morning, the news reports on the incident would be limited. But in a few hours, it would be a different story.

I opened the door to the family room adjacent to the master suite to find Ashur sipping scotch from a tumbler and sitting in a chair positioned at the corner of the room.

"Ashur."

"So, you're a Solon agent." The anger in Ashur's gaze gave me the urge to step back.

"For the time being I am," I said, taking a seat across from him.

A tick pulsed on the side of his face. "Then perhaps you should tell me when you plan to stop. 'Cause I'll be damned if I let my pregnant wife traipse around the world pointing guns at dictators."

"I didn't know I was pregnant. I would never have gone if I had known. I would never put our baby at risk."

"You should never have gone in the first place," he bellowed and then stood, moving to the window. "Now answer the question. When do you plan to stop?"

"I technically retired the day I returned from Pakistan."

"The way Tyler spoke, you're still his boss." He clenched his jaw when he said Tyler's name.

The fallout with Tyler was something I couldn't muster the energy to worry about at the moment. All I knew was Tyler's days as Secretary of State were probably numbered.

"So, which is it? Are you retired or active?"

"I guess active until the mess with the photos blows over." I grimaced inside. "If it blows over."

"When did they recruit you? The only way you go up the ranks of any military-based organization is if you worked your way up."

"It was the summer before I started law school at Stanford."

"So, was it Xander who recruited you?"

"Are you kidding me? Xander isn't part of Solon. He's..."

"MI6," Ashur finished. "And before you ask, he's part of a private operation I requested to help me locate a missing American ambassador to the United Nations who was kidnapped four months ago in Geneva."

"You knew what happened to Ame."

"Of course, I knew. Ameera Kamini is your best friend. She's been by your side from the moment we were engaged. I knew something had happened to her when she never took her flight back to New York."

"Why didn't you say anything?"

"Because I didn't want to scare you. I wanted to protect you. I'd hoped she'd be home before our wedding. Later I figured out you knew she was missing when you kept making excuses for her whereabouts. I suspected that you were working with one of your underground contacts to get her back."

"You were the third buyer."

He stayed quiet for a moment and then ran a hand down his face before he spoke. "People think I only see things in black and white. I knew what Ameera meant to you. I hoped if I could get Ameera back for you, then you'd see how much you meant to me. That you could trust me with your heart and secrets. Not just your body."

"Ash." I sighed and let the guilt and sadness of his words wash over me.

"Now I know it was a bullshit hope. You were never going to confide anything in me. Hell, you lived a double life." He released a resigned breath. "The irony of this whole debacle was that we were going to use money from the same account to bid on Ameera."

"Ashur, I'm so sorry."

"It's too late. What's the point in fighting for something that never was there in the first place?"

My lips trembled. "I want this to be real."

"What we have isn't real. It never was. It's better to stick to the contract. Give me my two children and I'll never bother you again."

CHAPTER TWENTY-ONE

I took a deep breath as I made my way to Ashur's office. I knew what I was about to do was right for all of us. I needed to leave town and take the spotlight off Ashur and his administration.

At first the news outlets believed the pictures were a hoax, then some began to question the various incidents I'd been involved in over the years. All the attention had also brought an uproar of anger and finger-pointing from Ashur's critics about what he knew regarding my past international work. There were threats of a federal inquiry.

Ashur hadn't said much about the accusation, except to release a statement questioning the validity of the pictures since I was pregnant and hadn't left the White House for weeks due to morning sickness. What surprised me most was the fact that the majority of Americans were more focused on a White House baby than the fact I may have been involved in an illegal international operation.

I knew I wasn't in the clear, but at least the heat on me wasn't as bad as it could have been. It was more the cold between Ashur and me that I couldn't live with any longer.

My dream of having a relationship with Ashur like the one my parents shared was long gone. The only hope I could have was one where we could peacefully tolerate each other.

I turned the corner and stopped in front of Leara's desk. "Is he in?"

"Go right in, Mrs. Kumar."

The guards opened the door before I approached and closed them once I passed over the threshold to the Oval Office.

"I wasn't expecting to see you," Ashur said as he set his pen down and pushed back from his desk.

"I know I'm the last person on this earth you want to see, but I had to give you this."

I set the revised contract on Ashur's desk with shaky hands.

He watched me with his penetrating gaze. "What it this?"

"It's something I should have done long ago." I stepped away from his desk.

He picked up the envelope and pulled out the papers.

After scanning them, he looked up. "What does this mean?"

"It means you're free." I bit my lip, swallowed, and squared my shoulders. "I'll leave for Seattle tomorrow."

"Why?"

"I can't live the way we've been living any longer and I know how you feel so I'm not sure what else is left to say."

"What about the baby?"

I covered my stomach. "I'd never keep you away from our children."

"The contract says two children." His words were cool but I felt the storm inside him.

I inhaled deeply, trying to hold in the tears burning the backs of my eyes. "I'm carrying twins, so I've met the requirements you stipulated."

"When did you find out?"

"During my appointment, the day after you learned my secrets." I closed my eyes for a second, trying to keep my emotions from overwhelming me.

"That was a week ago."

"I wasn't hiding the information from you. I wasn't sure how to bring it up when we haven't spent a single moment alone in the last seven days. And there is the fact you couldn't even look at me without anger."

"Tara."

"Don't, Ashur. I have to figure out my life. I promise I'll come back. No one will suspect what is going on between us. I'll be the dutiful first lady, but outside of that we'll continue to live separate lives as we've done for the last month."

"Are you going to stay with Solon?"

"Yes, but not in the same capacity as I did for the past ten years. I won't ever intentionally put my babies' lives in danger."

"Then what will you do?"

"It's classified."

A frown crossed his face, as well as irritation.

"All you need to know is that I won't be in the field. My role is more behind the scenes."

"I..." He hesitated, scratching a hand down his face. "I don't want you to leave."

"You don't get a vote. Now if we are done, I have a helicopter ready to take me to the airfield." My hand trembled as I tucked a lock of hair behind my ear.

I kept my composure when Hamir had held a gun to my head, not showing even an ounce of emotion, and now I was shaking like a leaf.

I could blame it on the pregnancy but I knew that would be a lie. I was accepting my fate. The one I'd created.

"So that's it?"

"Yes." I bit my lip as I turned to the door. I had to get out of the room or I'd lose it.

"Tara."

"What do you want from me, Ashur?"

"I wanted you to love me as much as I love you."

I gripped the doorknob and said over my shoulder, "I do. It never stopped for me. I know I was stupid to deny it, and I hurt you by keeping who I was a secret, but my only excuse was that I was protecting myself and countless others, including you."

"Then the money I offered you wasn't the reason you agreed to marry me?"

I shook my head. What point was there in denying something I'd known all along but refused to acknowledge?

"I used the excuse of money to justify wanting to marry you even with all our history." I wiped at the wetness streaming down my cheeks. "What does it matter? I fucked up. Now I know it's too late.

"The only thing I can promise is that the picture controversy will die down soon. I've spoken to the board in Geneva. They are going to release a statement through one of their Asian charities claiming the woman in the picture isn't me and they have no connection with me. The woman who posed as my decoy in past missions will be named as the unknown assassin. She's retiring and plans to assume a new identity so there won't be any blowback."

"So that's it?"

"What else is there? Our names will be cleared."

"I mean for us."

"I can't live this existence where we barely spend time

together outside of fucking. I need more of you than your body even if you think I don't deserve it." I took a deep breath and then said, "Goodbye, Ashu."

I opened the door and walked out.

Casey met me as I came down the hall from the Oval Office. His face was a wash of worry and concern.

"All my things on the copter?"

He nodded, following my brisk steps out of the residence. I had to get away as fast as possible before I completely fell apart.

"Mrs. Kumar, are you positive this is what you want to do? Is there no hope?"

"How would you feel if the woman you loved kept all the secrets I did?"

"You forget he married you under false pretenses too."

I snorted. "Not the same thing. He concocted his bargain as a way to get the woman he loved back."

"So did you. He's been the love of your life from the moment you mentioned your broken heart during your first-round training. The fact you worked for Solon had nothing to do with why you married him."

"I guess that all depends on how one views things."

I glanced behind me to the windows that lined the side wall of the Oval Office. Ashur stood there watching me. We held gazes for a few moments before he said something to someone and walked away.

My heart shattered.

And it ends. As of this moment, I'd live the life Ashur's parents lived. In public as a couple, but in private as strangers. The dream of having what Mummy and Dad had was no longer possible.

At least I'd have my babies. I rubbed the small swell of my belly.

Taking a deep, steadying breath, I waited for security to open the helicopter door so I could board, but instead the propellers slowed.

"What's going on?" I asked Casey, who looked as confused as I was.

"Let me see. You stay right here with Joel while I figure out what's going on." Casey walked toward the security building.

At that moment, two of Ashur's security approached me.

"Mrs. Kumar. Please come with us."

"Why?" I folded my arms. "I have a government plane waiting for me and the longer you delay me, the more it will cost the taxpayers."

The two men looked at each other as if they were scared of me.

"Please, ma'am. This is a direct order from the president."

An order. What the fuck could we have left to say?

"Is that right?" I glared at the agents who took a step away from me. "Fine, lead the way."

I stomped behind them until we reached Ashur's office.

The second the door opened, I stalked toward him, letting anger fill me instead of the sadness and tears floating under the surface of my composure. "What do you want? I'm exhausted and just want to go home."

"This is your home."

"No. My home is in Seattle."

"You sold your house, remember?"

"I'm going to stay in the lake house I had built for my parents. They won't mind me staying there."

"I don't want you to go." He searched my face. "Stay, Tara."

"Why? I don't fit here." I gestured to the area around us. "I don't have a purpose here. Give me one good reason why I should stay."

He grabbed my hand in his as I tried to poke him in the chest.

"Because you love me."

I tried to pull my hand away but his grip tightened.

"It's not enough."

"What about the fact I love you?"

I kept quiet.

"Then stay with me for my money. You see, in the last twenty minutes, my net worth doubled."

I clenched my jaw, glancing at the papers I'd given him thrown on a side table and bit out, "That is not funny."

"I'm not laughing, Tara. Do you know what it was like to see the details of that document? You gave me everything back, even the house I gave you as a wedding present."

"It didn't belong to me. You may have offered me the bargain as a way to get me back, but I accepted it without question. I got the easier end of the arrangement."

"Liar. Marrying me meant you tied yourself to me for life. It was far from the easier alternative." He ran a thumb along the skin of my wrist.

"My reasons don't matter. Please let me go." I tried to tug my arm free again but this time he laid it flat against his shirt. The heat of the skin underneath the fabric warmed through to my fingertips. "I can't do this, Ashur."

"Let me say this, and if you still feel like you have to leave then I'll let you go."

My shoulders slumped, and I resigned myself for whatever he had to tell me. If it would make it quicker for me to leave, then I'd do it.

"The press is right about me. You are my Achilles heel. You make me softer, kinder. You get me to be more flexible on issues I tend to view as black and white. I'm not the ridged asshole when you're around."

"Whatever. I don't have that kind of power over you."

"You have no idea. Half the Republicans think I've been brainwashed by my wife's feminine wiles. I'm no longer the conservative in Independent clothing that they voted for. I've sided with the Democrats on key issues and that is essentially telling them to fuck off. And the fact I don't give two shits about their opinion makes me an asshole."

"You're not an asshole. You just like people to think that so they're scared of you."

"No, baby." He cupped my face and it took all my will not to turn into the warmth of his palm. "You're the only one who thinks this. I can be an ass. Hell, I was an ass to you. Why do you think I was so angry with you? You held my heart in your hands and you crushed it. I tried to show you that you meant more to me than our agreement and you kept mentioning our contract. And then when I learned about Solon, I was more hurt that you kept a piece of yourself from me than the fact you were an agent for a secret organization."

"I never meant to hurt you."

"I know this now. Seeing the revised contract gutted me. You detailed all the duties you'd perform as a first lady as if it was a job description. It was so cold, and I'd thought our original contract was cold. You went so far as to state you'd agree to an annulment if you didn't meet the requirements of the agreement."

"I just wanted you to know I wouldn't shrug off my duties as your wife, even if we weren't really together."

"We are together. God, I'd give anything to get back what we had during our honeymoon." He dropped his forehead against mine. "I'm fucking this up. I'm not good with emotions. Maybe it was my upbringing or all the years I spent in the military, but I tend to be too serious."

"What are you saying?" My heart was beating so fast, it felt like it would explode out of my chest.

"That I don't want to do this without you. I love you, Tara. I need you."

I wanted to tell him that I needed him too, but held it back.

When I remained quiet, he tilted my chin up so he could stare into my tear-filled eyes.

"Say something, baby."

"I want to think this can work, but how will you deal with what I do? I am part of an organization whose sole purpose is to circumvent the law to achieve its goals."

"You make it sound like you're selling arms instead of trying to free people caught in the net of human trafficking."

"I'm serious. You have strict beliefs about what's right and wrong. Can you live with the fact I will constantly be looking for loopholes in US and international law for our efforts, while you are trying to uphold those laws? Being with me, could cost you your political career."

"Baby, I'm not sure if you realized this, but I'm not the squeaky-clean guy you think I am. I worked with your pal Xander under the radar and used my private funds to enter an illegal auction in a country that doesn't have the best relationship with the US. If anyone found out about that, what you did would be considered child's play.

"As for my political career," he continued, "I'd give it up without a thought if it meant I had you. Besides, it isn't as if I don't have another career waiting in the wings. Trust me, Tara. You wanted me to fight for you when we were younger and didn't. You have to know what I said the other night was bullshit. We do have something to fight for. I'm fighting for you now."

I stared at him, trying to process all that he'd said.

Tears spilled down my face.

He'd put his reputation on the line not for the sole purpose of saving Ameera, but for me. He loved me so much that he'd set his strict rules to the side. I'd wanted him to fight for me and he'd done it in a way that I could never have expected.

He'd tried over and over to tell me how he felt about me and I pushed it away, fearing what the future would bring, but I had no future without him. He was it for me. Always had been. Always would be.

"Say something."

His amber gaze pleaded with me, breaking the last of my resistance. I wiped the dampness from my cheeks and then touched his face.

He released an apprehensive breath and asked, "Are you in?"

I nodded, lifting my lips to his. "I'm in."

"Thank God." He fisted my hair and returned my kiss.

My body immediately responded with the need and desire I'd tried to push away. I wrapped my arms around his shoulders as he cupped my ass, lifting me against him.

"I love you," I murmured against his mouth. "You're the only man I have ever love and will love."

He broke our kiss and smiled. "You have no idea how long I've waited for you to say it."

"I promise to tell you every day for the rest of our lives, Mr. President."

"I look forward to it, First Lady."

THE END

ABOUT THE AUTHOR

Inspired by her years working in corporate America, Sienna loves to serve up stories woven around confident and successful women who know what they want and how to get it, both in – and out – of the bedroom.

Her heroines are fresh, well-educated, and often find love and romance through atypical circumstances. Sienna treats her readers to enticing slices of hot romance infused with empowerment and indulgent satisfaction.

Sienna loves the life of travel and adventure. She plans to visit even the farthest corners of the world and delight in experiencing the variety of cultures along the way. When she isn't writing or traveling, Sienna is working on her "happily ever after" with her husband and children.

Sign up for her newsletter to be notified of releases, book sales, events and so much more.
www.SiennaSnow.com

facebook.com/authorsiennasnow

twitter.com/sienna_snow

instagram.com/bysiennasnow

bookbub.com/authors/sienna-snow

Reckless Romeo (A Cocky Hero Club Novel)

<u>Wicked Kings</u>

Coming Fall 2020